The Passage

BRUCE NICOLAYSEN

SPHERE BOOKS LIMITED
30/32 Gray's Inn Road, London WC1X 8JL

First published in Great Britain
by Sphere Books Ltd 1979
Copyright © Bruce Nicolaysen 1976

TRADE MARK

Printed in Great Britain by
C. Nicholls & Company Ltd
The Philips Park Press, Manchester

For my daughters,
Kjirsti and Inger

"We journey through space and time; every day is a passage of our body and our soul."

PERILOUS PASSAGE

1

The wolf died quickly. One instant he was a whole wolf, and the next he was several pieces of wolf being ripped savagely into smaller pieces by the knife teeth of two huge jaws.

They had chased him before, these two shaggy white dogs from another land, strangers, interlopers with the smell of death about them, *Komondorok* from the mountain wilds of Hungary. Standing thirty inches across the shoulder and weighing one hundred and thirty pounds each, a Komondor was a fierce guardian of sheep, a killer of any wolf in the Pyrenees.

The wolf had not intended to fight with them. He was an old gray muzzle who had learned the ways of sheep and dogs, living off the first while avoiding the other. These *Komondorok* had trailed him many times, and he had always escaped because if he was not as strong, he was faster, wilier, and knew the mountain terrain better.

But this time his wolf memory lapsed, and he ran into a stony ravine that narrowed until the rock walls towered far above his jumping powers, and the rock walls became the sides of his tomb.

He whirled about to face the dogs, his hind legs sweeping through the air in an arc, his front legs the pivot point, his hair bristling and standing straight out from his neck and back. The skin of his lips pulled back, and saliva drooled over his teeth and down the gray muzzle. He was defiant, savage, ready to fight, unwilling to die easily, but too old and too wise not to know that this ravine had become his bone yard.

When the wolf turned, the dogs paused for the briefest moment. Then they touched each other's shoulder as a signal and charged. There was no deception, not even great speed, simply a barrage of power, and the first dog bowled the wolf over as the second dog took out his throat.

The wolf was already dead but did not know it, and the first dog came back and crunched his teeth through the wolf's skull until the bone splintered and the carcass fell away from the skull, which was in the clamp of teeth, mingled with saliva, blood, and the last whined rage of death. The first dog sat down and watched while the second began licking the red patch of blood that stained the matted white hair of his chest. Suddenly they bristled and turned to investigate the sounds coming down the ravine. It was a man. They caught his scent, and their hair settled back.

He was their master. A Basque with the hardy body of a mountain man and a face made ageless by solitude and the softness of the morning mists. From a little distance he could be thirty or fifty. In fact, he was thirty-eight.

His clothing was dark and heavy; handmade. The shirt was buttoned to the top to ward off the cold, but the jacket he left open for better movement. Dark, unpressed trousers covered the tops of thick-soled mountain boots.

It was an old sheep killer, he thought when he saw the gray muzzle, an old killer who had lived off the work of others for many years. He was a shepherd. A hater of wolves. He spit on the carcass and started out of the ravine.

One of the huge *Komondorok* looked up as if to say, "Well, it was a good piece of work, was it not?" But the Basque pushed him aside with his heavy boot and went on. The dogs followed.

They passed a jumble of rocks that many ages ago had tumbled down from a higher point on the mountain; bulky, gray shapes cracked and tossed down by the winds and rains and glaciers; the same gray rocks that had burst through the skin of the earth when the Pyrenees had been born.

The Basque, oblivious to the rock fall, came to his house. It was made of stone, the cracks chinked with mud and straw to keep out the howling winter winds, the roof pitched at a steep angle to shed the snow. The sheep pens came right up to the barn, which was attached to the house. He checked the wooden gate before he went into the house. It was a sturdy gate with posts twice the thickness of a man's arm. He had carved it himself. He had made the fence himself. Everything he had built himself and had no need or use for anyone else. He looked to see if the dogs had taken up their places near the pen and, satisfied, closed the door behind him.

The *Komondorok* had been an expense, a great expense, but he had fearfully paid the money to the Frenchman, who claimed they were supposedly the best guard dogs in the world. The ordinary Spanish sheep dogs, while excellent herders, were not ferocious enough, and the huge Great Pyrenees dogs were too placid by nature. He needed *killers*. Dogs who needed little, could stand any weather, and would never forget their duties. *Komondorok* were perfect. They never left the flock. They never entered the cabin, never whimpered in the cold, never whined in the rain. And while their long, white hair grew tangled and matted, they knew their job and would attack any man, beast, or devil who bothered the sheep.

The Basque ate his supper in silence, a version of paella with bits of lamb, pimento, saffron rice, and green beans cooked in a thick sauce. From time to time he lifted a *chahakoa* and expertly squirted a stream of bitter white wine into his mouth. When he was done, he put his few dishes in the wooden barrel that was half filled with water, lit his pipe, sat down on a hard chair, and stared straight ahead.

His name was Erno Urquijo, and his head, with its broadness at the temples tapering to a narrow, squared chin, was a common type among Basques. His upper body was large, building from a hard, flat waist through a barrel chest to strong, wide shoulders. His hair was dark and shaggy and curled over the top of his shirt collar. His black moustache was turning gray. His face was tanned the deep bronze of a mountain man; a tan that has burned in so deeply it will never fade. On top of his head he wore the inevitable beret.

Years ago, in times buried in the corner of his memory, he had lived in a village of scrubbed white houses with red tile roofs and handsomely carved wooden balconies. Erno Urquijo had lived in such a house for years, but now he was through with it all. The talk. The parades of men in red berets and white trousers. The musicians playing "Titi Biliti." The sappers with axes on their shoulders, wearing fur caps and false beards, girded in white leather aprons. Fat women selling *rosquillos*, crisp baked dough sprinkled with sugar. Old hags selling ducks and geese, their shoes gray with the dust of the road. The young girls laughing and telling breathless secrets to one another. It was all in the past.

He had been married then, and in love. And it had all been taken away from him. Cruelly. By other men. And that was why he had no desire to live with other men. There had been an argument in the tavern, and the argument turned into a question of honor, and knives flashed. The brawl spilled out of the tavern and into the street, where Erno's wife was walking. The girl was terrified and tried to flee, but she crossed the street as a knife was thrown and, unluckily, took the full force of the blade in her back. The men who were fighting stopped, and everyone stood around, scuffing the ground with the toes of their boots, looking foolish and unhappy and ashamed of what they had done.

Erno never said a word. He carried the body of his wife into the mountains. He marked the little grave with a tombstone bearing the sun symbol, a symbol that reached back across the millennia, across the hundreds of generations of Basques to the origins of their race, now lost in the mists of time.

The man who had thrown the knife died mysteriously in his sleep. A great rock had fallen and crushed his skull. The authorities never questioned where the rock came from. It was fate, and it was a waste of time to question fate.

Erno moved into the mountains and built his cabin. He raised sheep and came to the village only to sell wool and buy supplies. His wife had died in 1930. Ten years ago. He never forgot and never forgave.

He cared more for the dung of his sheep than the people of the village.

His cabin had become his only source of pride, his own version of a family seat. It was his share in the heritage of the *Eskual-Herria*—the Basque fatherland—and he lived alone in it, aware of his identity and independence. Identity to a Basque was important. They had kept themselves separate and distinct even during the hundreds of years when the Africans and Moors had left traces of their blood and culture in the French and Spanish peoples. Although a Basque might live in Spain, he did not consider himself a Spaniard any more than a Basque on the French side considered himself a Frenchman. The *Eskual-Herria* was a thing unto itself and spread through the mountains to the sea, covering a part of Spain and a part of France and admitting identity with neither. As a political factor, there no longer was a Basque nation, only the Basques and the Basque soul, which was enough.

There were no books in the cabin, no radio because the mountains would block the signals; besides, there was nothing he wanted to hear. The only furnishings in the house were for use. A table with his pipes and carving knives. Some chairs. An elaborate, hand-carved wooden bed that had belonged to his mother. There was a stand for cooking utensils. One corner of the room was given over to his current project, at this time the gardening tools he was repairing after a season of use.

He smoked until his pipe died out, gave it a final tap, and set it down on the table. It was time to get to work.

He picked up a sickle, a beautiful tool, extending the length and usefulness of a man's arm, and began sharpening it with a whetstone. The sickle gave off a ringing sound that filled the cabin. He worked slowly and methodically, taking care to give each portion of the blade the correct number of strokes, making sure the sharpness would be equal along its full length.

The dogs outside growled, and he heard footsteps on the dirt path. There was a knock at the door. With a low mutter not very different from the growling of his dogs, he went to the door and opened it.

There were two men. He recognized one, a man named Perea, from the village of Reduna, which was in a valley several miles away. The Basque was as friendly to him as he was with the rest of the villagers, which was not at all.

"What do you want?" the Basque asked, and before the man could answer, he added, "I am busy."

"Many pardons for the interruption, but my friend and myself have come to talk to you about a business proposition." He spoke a curious French, obviously not his native tongue but spoken for the benefit of his companion, who spoke neither Basque nor Spanish.

The Basque thought for a moment, then finally opened the door wider and allowed the men to enter. The man from the village, Perea, was several years younger than the Basque and handsome. He wore a brown wool coat with white piping, corduroy trousers, and a beret pulled to one side of his head. His boots were heavy leather, not the usual rope-soled shoes of the men of the Pyrenees.

"This is urgent," he said.

The Basque grunted. No one ever came to his cabin because no one was welcome. He wanted them to get out. They smelled of a world he had no interest in, but Perea had mentioned a matter of business, and one had to be interested in profit.

Perea introduced his companion. "This is Renoudot.

He is French." He paused and then said, "We are working with people who have interests in Spain and France. All of Europe, in fact."

The Basque said nothing. The man would get to the business proposition soon enough, and he could accept it or, which was more likely, reject it and get back to his sickle.

"We want you to help us get some people through the mountains."

There it was, the piece of business.

"What people?"

"Four people who are in France. We want to bring them through the mountains. They cannot come through passes because the authorities check everyone, and these people cannot be seen."

"They are criminals?"

Perea smiled. "Yes, in a way, they are criminals. But the people who call them that are the Germans who criminally stole France. So, in another way, they are not criminals."

The Frenchman spoke for the first time. "No one who is against the Nazis is a criminal."

The Basque said nothing. He had heard there was another war starting in Europe. He had heard the Germans had defeated the French. All of this had caused a rush of smuggling over the border, though his particular part of the mountains saw little because the terrain was rough and forbidding.

"Crossing the mountains here is difficult."

"That's why it is a good place," Perea said. "The Germans and the Vichy guards don't watch the border too closely since they think no one could make it."

"They are right."

"You have never crossed?"

The Basque scratched the side of his head. "Yes, I have

crossed. In summer the sheep wander, and I go after them."

Perea turned to the Frenchman and nodded. This was the man for the job.

"I have no interest in this," the Basque said.

Perea nodded. The bargaining was commencing. "We are not asking you to do this without payment. Two thousand pesetas for going to France and bringing the people back."

"Who will tend my sheep when I am away?"

"It will only be a few days. Less than a week."

This was something to consider. He could leave food, and the sheep would be all right for a week. The dogs would guard them. He had left the sheep alone before, once for ten days, and nothing had happened.

"Two thousand pesetas is not enough. I want ten thousand."

The Frenchman became angry.

"These are people's lives you are arguing about!"

"Their lives are not my concern. You ask me to leave my sheep, and I am taking a chance that something might happen. You must pay me well to do that."

Perea agreed. "You are right. But ten thousand pesetas! We are not rich. We will pay you five thousand."

The Basque considered the new offer for a minute. He said, "Five thousand. Very well. But I will not be gone more than a week, and you must pay me now."

Without a word the men pulled up chairs and sat down around the table. The bargain had been made, and now only the details had to be settled. Perea counted out five thousand pesetas and gave them to the Basque, who stuffed them in his pocket without a glance.

They discussed their plans. The three of them would start through the mountains tomorrow, and by the second night they should reach St. Limoux on the other side. From there the Basque and Renoudot would take a train to Toulouse.

"Toulouse!" the Basque said. "That is far."

"About a hundred kilometers from St. Limoux, but the train is fast and takes only a few hours."

"Why must we go to Toulouse?"

"Because the four people are there, waiting for us. You will come back to St. Limoux by train, and all of us will come back across the mountains."

"Why do you not go to Toulouse?"

"Because fewer people attract less atention. Besides, I am staying in St. Limoux to get clothes and supplies for the people."

"How long will we be in Toulouse?"

"Overnight. But that is the easy part. It is the mountain crossing that is difficult. That is why we need you."

"It is getting cold up here. Snow is coming."

"People who are running from a bullet do not worry about the cold," the Frenchman said.

The Basque did not like him. If you didn't do what he did and believe what he believed, Renoudot thought you a fool. He didn't even realize that all this was a great imposition. Perea, at least, understood that. Perea, who had lived all his life with Basques and adopted many of their ways, knew that much.

It was a great deal of trouble, but five thousand pesetas was a great deal of money.

"We will go at dawn," the Basque said.

He blew out the lamp and went to his bed. He did not offer to show the others where to sleep. They went near the fire and lay down on the floor.

Once during the night the *Komondorok* made a racket and chased after something in the woods. The Basque awoke, listened for a moment, and then, hearing the dogs return, went back to sleep.

2

It was before first light, and the men were awake.

They fried salt cod in a pan, and the cabin filled with perfume from the sea. They ate quickly and silently. The Basque scrubbed his plate in the tub of water near the fire and went outside to tend his sheep. They came out of their sheds and crowded around him as he worked, their warm steamy bodies rubbing against him. They were *churra* sheep, marked with the red dye on the left flank that identified their owner. Although their wool was not as fine a clip as the merino, nor as valuable, they were a sturdier lot and survived better in the higher altitudes.

There was a stream with water. There was fodder and silage. The Basque filled the bins with dried grass. He patted a few heads. With the dogs to guard them, they would be all right for a week.

"The light is coming," he said to the men waiting at the fire. "We will need all the light we can get to make the trip in two days."

The closer hills loomed black against the lightening blue of the sky, and the breath of the men steamed in front of their faces. The light came up rapidly, and it was the new day.

The men started along an ancient stock path and were swallowed up in the hills covered with forests of Spanish chestnut, oak, elm, beech, and pine.

They had come about two hundred meters from the cabin when the Basque stopped. "Wait here," he said, and left the path.

He climbed over a fallen tree trunk. His foot scraped the side, and the rotten bark crumbled into powder and fell slowly to the earth. He walked around a large boulder and stopped. A slab of stone with a sun symbol carved on it was standing in the ground.

He looked down and tried to see the defining lines between his wife's grave and the adjoining earth but could not. It had become one, earth into earth, with the scrubby little plants scattered on top of what once had been fresh, raw dirt. Time had erased the memory of a last resting place, identified now only by the stone slab. Eventually the slab would be gone, but that would take reaches of time far longer than the short span of a man's life. The monument would outlive the maker.

The Basque stared at the grave for a long time. He did not pray, did not move. Finally he noticed the other men watching, and without a backward glance he returned to the path and began climbing again.

The stock path ended, the last sign of man's presence, and they picked their way through the hills. The Basque seemed to know every rock and tree. He avoided the denser brush that grew at the bottoms of ravines and spared them the trouble of climbing over crests. He went surely and directly along ways with the best footing and easiest climbing. Occasionally, when they broke into a clearing, they could look up and see the snowcapped peaks of the giants, and once they passed near a cirque, one of those unique formations found in the Pyrenees, a round amphitheater carved into the limestone, its sides carrying cascades of freezing water born in the snow on the crests.

They stopped for rest and food when the sun was at its highest in the sky, but the Basque seemed moody and not interested in conversation, so the men spent the time in silence. They continued their journey after lunch.

Once, when they came over the top of a small ridge, Perea started to follow what looked like the easiest path, but the Basque touched his shoulder, shook his head, and pointed in another direction.

Perea did not understand until a few minutes later, when they had climbed higher, and he could look back. The easy-looking path ended in a pile of fallen rocks at the base of an almost sheer cliff. If they had followed the easy-looking path, they would have been forced to turn back.

Perea looked at the Basque guide in admiration. The man knew the mountains.

Later in the day, when the sky began to darken, and they were buried deep in the high range, they came to a crevasse with an old, rotten log thrown across as a bridge. The Basque went first, carefully feeling his way with each step. The crevasse was only about six feet across, but the abyss below extended for several hundred feet.

Perea went next. The first two steps were without mishap, and then the toe of his heavy boot slid, and Perea fell forward onto the log, which immediately groaned and began to give way beneath him. With a desperate lunge he pushed himself forward and fell into the waiting arms of the Basque.

The heavy log groaned again and then slipped and clattered and smashed its way down the sides of the cliff until at last it hit the distant bottom, the rotten wood shattering and splintering to bits.

Perea looked down. He turned to the Basque, who was also looking down at the log. "Thank you."

The Basque said nothing. He looked across the crevasse at Renoudot.

The Frenchman was staring down into the hole. Beads of perspiration began forming on his forehead. Finally he looked away.

"Jump. I will catch you," Perea said.

Renoudot stood frozen on the spot.

"It is only a small jump. I will catch you," Perea said, this time glancing at the Basque. There was a look of contempt on the shepherd's face. Without a word he took the long length of rope he had been carrying and uncurled part of it. He took a piton from his pack and drove it into the rock face. He slipped the end of the rope through the piton and tested the strength of the hold. The piton dug into the rock and held.

The Basque walked to the edge of the crevasse and tossed the rope across to Renoudot. The Frenchman looked at it without understanding.

"Tie it around yourself," the Basque said.

Renoudot bent over and picked up the end of the rope and tied it around his middle. His hands trembled.

The Basque slipped more rope through the piton and then looked at Renoudot. "Jump. If you fall, I will catch you."

Renoudot nodded. He crossed himself and stood at the edge of the hole. He looked down and then away. The

'Basque, for the first time, became irritated. "Jump, damn it."

The Frenchman took a deep breath, closed his eyes, and started to jump. His nerve failed just as he was pushing off. His body collapsed, and he fell forward, his momentum carrying him to the other side but far too low; his hands struck the rock face, and he screamed and began to fall.

The Basque whipped the rope through the piton and let Renoudot fall about forty meters before he began to take in the slack of the rope wrapped about his body. Renoudot continued to scream even as his fall braked, slowed, and finally came to a stop; the scream changed to a sob as he dangled on the end of a rope sixty meters below.

The Basque muttered an oath and began to pull Renoudot up. Perea leaped forward and helped haul in the line. Within minutes Renoudot was pulled over the top to safety. He stood panting for a few seconds before he had enough courage to look at the other two men.

"I . . . I'm sorry," he managed to say.

The Basque said nothing as he recoiled the rope and brought it back over his shoulder. He turned and resumed climbing without seeming to notice the presence of the other two.

As the last light of day was fading, the Basque turned from the path and brought them to a small grotto with two openings. They built a fire and cooked their dinner.

After eating, the Basque lit his pipe and for the first time began a conversation. "Are you convinced of the difficulty of crossing here?"

Perea nodded. "It is difficult, but we are crossing."

"The sky holds snow."

"That will make it more difficult?"

"Difficult, impossible, who knows?"

"Will it snow tomorrow?"

"I don't think so. In any event, it will be easier tomorrow. The country is rougher, but it is mostly downhill. It is easier going this way, more difficult from the other side.

"We are over on the other side?"

"By midmorning we will pass the crest, and from there you will look down into France."

"France," Renoudot said, starting to get up.

"Are you going now?" The Basque seemed amused. "It would take you hours, and you would break your leg in the darkness."

Perea was thinking. "You know exactly where we are. You must have known about this grotto."

"Yes."

"You have stayed here before?"

"Yes. It is a good place to stay. Tonight it is clear, but it rains much up here. The French side of the mountains wrings much of the water from the wind before it gets to Spain."

Renoudot walked to the opening of the grotto and looked up at the sky. After a time he said, "A million worlds and here we must crawl through the hills to save people who are forbidden to occupy a single square foot of ground."

The Basque looked puzzled. "What are you talking about?"

"The fact that men do senseless things. Things without a purpose."

The Basque shook his head. "You make no sense. What has no purpose? I am getting paid five thousand pesetas for this work. Is that not a purpose?" The Basque stared at him suspiciously. "How much do you get paid?"

Perea threw the stub of his cigarette into the fire. "Nothing. We do this because it must be done."

"Nothing!" the Basque said in surprise.

He did not believe it. They must be lying. There had to be a trick. They didn't want him to know they were making more money than he was. That was it.

"I must have another thousand pesetas."

"Why?"

"It is more difficult than I thought."

"But we made a bargain."

"And now we make another bargain."

"But that is impossible."

"Another thousand or I go back."

Perea understood. "You do not believe we are doing this for nothing, is that it? You think we are cheating you and giving you a smaller share?"

The Basque said nothing.

"But it is the truth. We are paid nothing."

"If it is the truth, then you are crazy, and I want another thousand pesetas because I must travel with madmen."

Perea said no more. He took out his note case, counted out a thousand pesetas, and gave them to the Basque.

"Perhaps someday you will understand why men help other men for nothing."

The Basque grunted. Men smuggled for money. It made no difference what they smuggled. Tobacco, whiskey, horses, or people. It was a business with risk, and one was paid well to do it.

He opened his pack and took out an oilskin, lay on it, and drew the ends about himself. It was a crazy conversation; tomorrow would be a hard day, and a man needed rest.

*   *   *

In the iciness of the morning on the mountain slope, the men stood in a sea of mist as they plunged their hands under the waterfall and sucked the crystal-clear water. Their hands tingled.

They left the grotto and climbed. In several hours they reached a crest and could see no more high mountains in front of them. France, a series of foothills after a long drop from the crest, descending into a patchwork of cultivated fields, disappeared in the haze of distance. The Frenchman made the sign of the cross and murmured a short prayer

As the Basque had promised, the journey was mostly downhill, and they went from ravine to ravine, along the banks of streams, and through narrow defiles. The brush was thicker and the way down very steep, and each of them knew it would be a more difficult climb coming back.

Once the Basque stopped and peered intently up a ravine at a small, heavily timbered hill.

"What do you see?" Perea asked.

"Nothing, but there is a hermit living up there."

"A hermit," Perea said. "Do you know him?"

"No. I talked with him years ago. Maybe he is dead now. I do not know. He would not want to see us, anyway. He came here to be alone."

"How does he live?" the Frenchman asked.

"Small animals, roots, herbs, whatever there is. It is enough. A man can live off the mountains, depending on what is enough for the man. *Asko badok, asko bearkodok,* " he said, quoting the Basque proverb—if you want much, you'll always lack much.

"How long has he lived here?"

"He did not tell me. I followed a lost sheep and found it with a broken leg under a tree. I killed it, and he appeared and asked if he could have it. He was pleased enough by the gift to talk. The first time in years, he said."

"But why did he come here in the first place?" the Frenchman asked.

The Basque looked at him and said nothing. He pushed his *makhila*—a heavy walking stick tipped with iron—into the earth and continued down the hill. They talked no more for the rest of the day.

The land began to curve flat.

They were at the base of the range, and the sun was disappearing from the sky. As they walked the miles to St. Limoux, Perea broke the long silence and explained his plan. "The two of you will take the train to Toulouse and stay there for the night. Tomorrow, you and the four people will take the late-afternoon train back here. On the following morning we all go back into the mountains."

"Why not an early train tomorrow morning?" the Basque asked. "I must get back to my sheep."

"There is no train in the morning. Besides, it is better to travel at night."

"Why?"

"Less chance of being seen."

"I must get back to my sheep."

Perea looked at the Basque in helpless anger. "If you get caught, you will *never* get back to your sheep!"

They fell into silence as they passed through a small village. The houses and dirt streets differed little from the villages on the other side of the mountains—a village inn, a few shops, a handful of houses.

Finally they reached St. Limoux—a country village that was little more than a train station and a dozen shops. Renoudot stopped in front of a small stone house, went inside, and in a moment reappeared with the owner, Andres, their local contact. After everyone solemnly shook hands, Perea and Andres went inside the house, and the other two went down the street to the depot.

The train was already in the station, an old, patched-up locomotive, two passenger cars, and three freight cars. The bawling of sheep came from the last car, and the Basque started down to inspect them, but Renoudot took his arm and indicated it was time to board.

It was filthy inside, the floor littered with trash, with a sour smell of bodies and rotting food. There were no compartments, only row after row of seats. Half the car's compartments were filled with peasants. The other compartments were filled with French soldiers talking loudly and passing around a bottle of wine. The soldiers were Vichy, collaborators of the Germans.

Renoudot and the Basque slipped into a pair of seats at the back. The Frenchman handed over a set of forged papers that described Urquijo as a Basque living in a small village on the French side of the mountains. No one would question it. A Basque was a Basque. Even the Germans understood that.

The Basque looked at the picture, which was glued to the papers. It was not he, but someone who looked a great deal like him.

"Who is this man?"

"I don't know. Perea obtained it."

Perea must have felt quite sure of himself when he came to the cabin, the Basque thought. If I had known that, I might have raised my price.

The conductor came and collected the fares, hardly glancing at the two men in their rough clothes. If they had been well dressed, they would have merited closer scrutiny. The conductor was loyal to the new government. Only last week he had uncovered a traitor making his way toward the mountains. The officer of gendarmes who came for the man had some very nice things to say. Perhaps they would send him a letter. He would frame it and hang it on the wall in his home. That would be a proud thing to have.

The Basque slept. He did not dream and woke instantly when Renoudot shook his arm. The train was coming into the *Gare Matabiau*, the main railroad station in Toulouse. A long troop train had stopped, and thousands of German soldiers were climbing from the boxcars, stiff, dust-covered, travel-weary. They lit cigarettes, stretched their arms, and spit. A few urinated on the heavy iron wheels of the cars.

The Basque and Renoudot were walking past a freight train when the shepherd noticed the doors of the cars were chained. Slits opened along the sides, and he could see eyes peering out. He almost stopped but kept going when he saw there was a uniformed guard on top of each car. The Germans were taking no chances with the people inside.

Hearing the footsteps, the prisoners began calling out to the passengers from St. Limoux.

"Water . . . please . . . water . . ."

"For the love of God, please . . ."

"My son, his tongue is black!"

"Water . . ."

"I had a house and they burned it. . . ."

"Please . . . water . . ."

"Water . . . I will pay . . ."

"I have a diamond ring. I will pay a diamond ring for water, a diamond ring!"

One of the Vichy soldiers, drunk, unable to walk a straight line, went over and peered through a slit.

"What is that you are saying, m'sieu? Water? You want water?"

The German guard on top of the car shouted out in

rage, "Get back! Get back! It is forbidden! Forbidden! Forbidden to come near! Forbidden!"

He shouted in German, but if the Vichy soldier did not understand the words, there was no mistaking the tone nor the menacing gesture with the machine gun. He backed off and stumbled away with his friends.

After that the peasants did not even look at the cars but kept their eyes on the path in front of them.

They passed through the station, and it was filled with a bustling crowd. Soldiers carrying heavy packs and rifles, clumping across the floor, looking tired as soldiers always do when weighted down with the tools of their trade. Peasants staggering under immense loads, groaning their way from one place to another. German officers, resplendent in gray uniforms and curved caps, lolling around, looking down their noses at the commotion of the station, the filth, the rags of the peasants, the *Frenchness* of it all.

Renoudot and the Basque walked for a mile, and the Basque was impressed with the long blocks of red brick buildings. He had never believed the stories of the rich Basques who were supposed to live here in marble palaces, but from the size and richness of what he saw, he began to think they might be true.

Suddenly an open-topped automobile carrying four policemen passed them, its tires squealing as it turned into a side street. Instinctively Renoudot moved into the shadow of the building, but the police had no interest in the two men. They screeched to a halt in front of a small house, and all four got out of the car and ran into the house. Inside the house, there was a great deal of shouting, the sounds of fighting, the terrified scream of a woman.

The policemen reappeared dragging a man who kept

struggling to break free. On the sidewalk two policemen held him while another smashed him across the bridge of the nose with a heavy, lead-filled club. There was a sharp crack, and the man's face seemed to explode, a piece of pulp with blood pouring over the face. The man collapsed on the pavement. A woman ran out of the house, hysterical, pushing past the police, falling on the injured man.

At this moment a German staff car came down the street, preceded by two motorcycles. The Basque and Renoudot began to move on.

They arrived at their destination, a four-story brick house with cracked wooden cornices. All the shades were pulled down. Renoudot knocked at the door.

It opened. The painted face of an aging woman looked out.

"Oh, it's you," she said when she saw Renoudot.

She peered beyond them into the quiet street. Satisfied that they were alone, she held the door open, and the men went inside.

The Basque looked in wonder at the hallway. The walls had colored murals, interrupted every few feet by wide, full-length mirrors. A thick, worn carpet stretched the length of the hall, and he could hear voices coming from a room that opened onto it.

The lighting was hushed, subdued, casting a reddish hue. The Basque felt warmed by it. Never in his life had he seen the like of it.

"You must get those people out of here," the woman said to Renoudot. "If they were captured, it would be the end of me."

"Tomorrow."

The woman shook her head in disgust. "This minute would not be soon enough."

"The arrangements are for tomorrow."

She turned and started down the hall. "This way. They are upstairs in the back of the attic."

Her silk dress made a swish-swishing sound, and her high heels caused her broad hips to swing from side to side. The Basque looked on approvingly. They passed the room with the open door, and he saw several women, painted, plump, dressed in revealing, colorful dresses. Several men were with them. They were well dressed and groomed. One wore a uniform of a Vichy officer. This was not a place of peasants.

A woman in a low-cut purple gown passed the officer, and he patted her on the rump. She laughed, a low, gravelly laugh, and came over and put her arm about his neck.

The Basque stopped, but Renoudot tugged on his arm and made him go on.

They came to the end of the hall, and the woman opened a door and pointed to a small staircase. "All the way to the top and then to the right. There is a partition, and they are behind it."

She walked away, and once again the Basque admired her. When she was gone, he followed the Frenchman up the staircase.

"What is this place?"

"What do you think? A house of prostitutes."

The Basque nodded. "They are attractive."

"We are here on business. You are paid to tend to it."

"Perhaps there is time for everything."

They came to the top of the stairs and entered the darkened attic. A light crept from beneath a low door.

Renoudot knocked.

There was a slight noise from behind the door and then silence.

"Someone is in there," Renoudot whispered, and knocked again. It was met with silence.

Renoudot turned the handle and slowly opened the door.

At first the Basque saw only two men at a small table. The older wore delicate gold-rimmed eyeglasses; the other appeared to be a boy, fourteen or fifteen years old. Then he saw the woman in the corner, her hands folded in her lap, her eyes looking fearfully at a mattress in the corner. From under a blanket on the mattress a girl's face peeked out, half hidden by disheveled black hair, her pretty face made softer by sleep.

"We are friends," Renoudot said, and motioned the Basque into the room. "We have come to take you over the mountains."

The older woman mumbled something in a strange language, and the Basque peered at her.

"This is Professor Isaac Bergman, his wife, his son, and daughter," Renoudot said to the Basque. He turned to the others. "Permit me to introduce myself, I am Renoudot. And this gentleman is a guide who will take us through the mountains."

"I am happy to meet you, sir," the man said formally.

The Basque looked at the refugees, his face flushing with anger. "Are these the ones you expect me to take across the mountains?"

"Yes."

"Women. Children. A thin, weak man. These are the ones you expect to cross through the mountains?"

"Yes, I told you."

"No, I tell *you!* They will not make it. They could never cross. I will not go with them. They will die."

"We will die if we remain here," the older man said.

The mother began to cry, and the boy went over to her side. He limped as he walked.

"A cripple! You expect a cripple to climb over the back of the Pyrenees?"

The Basque began to raise his voice. These people were soft, terrified, cringing weaklings who would fall down and cry out on the torturous trails of the mountains. They could never make the journey. Perea had played him for a fool!

"If they could cross at all, it would take a month, and my sheep would be dead."

"It will not take a month, and these people will be dead if they stay here."

"They are not my concern. I have my sheep to think of."

Renoudot looked ready to fight, and Professor Bergman stepped between the men, turning to the Basque. "We are desperate, sir. We need help, and you have my promise we will be no trouble. If, when we get to the mountains, we cause inconvenience, I will be the last to blame you if you leave us."

The Basque smiled grimly. "Leave the four of you alone in the mountains? With the snow beginning and the wind cutting to the bone? Do you know what it is like to be lost in the dark? To stumble and fall and feel every breath of air cut like a knife through your lungs? You would die if I left you."

"We will die if we remain here. Perhaps it will be a better death in the quiet and beauty of the mountains."

The Basque pointed to the woman. "Do you think she is strong enough to climb mountains?" He pointed to the boy. "Do you think that one with the bad leg can jump across streams, climb over rocks, and walk all day?"

"My wife and son will do the best they can."

The older woman spoke again in the strange language.

"What is she saying?" the Basque asked. "What language is that?"

"Yiddish."

The Basque thought for a moment. Ah-ha, so that was it. Jews! "Listen, Jew, why should I risk my life for you?"

"We are not asking you to risk your life, sir. The moment we become a burden, you may leave us."

"Besides, a bargain has been made, and you have been well paid," Renoudot said.

"Well paid, well paid!" the Basque said, his anger rising. The veins on his forehead stood out. His mouth grew tighter. "Not for this have I been well paid! I must have what I first asked for—ten thousand pesetas. I want the other four thousand. Now!"

"I haven't got that much. Perea has the money."

The Basque turned to Bergman. "Do you have money?"

"Only a few francs."

"Give them to me."

"I have friends who will pay what you ask."

"I want whatever money you have right now."

Bergman took out a few notes and handed them to the Basque. "I promise my friends will make up the difference."

The Basque looked at the money in his hand. It was nothing, only a few francs. He shoved it in his pocket and spit on the floor. "Not enough. Perea must give me four thousand pesetas before we go back into the mountains. Four thousand more, do you understand?"

Renoudot nodded wearily. "I give you my word that Perea will pay you. Now you must agree to take these people."

"Yes, but it is crazy. I will leave them a few hours after we have gone into the mountains."

"Then Perea and myself will get them through."

The Basque said nothing. Perea and this Frenchman could never get them through. They would get lost and be lucky if they made it through themselves. But that was their business. He would cross through the mountains, and anyone who could stay with him would live.

"It is late. I am going downstairs with the women. Tomorrow be ready on time. I must get back to my sheep."

He went out, leaving the door open, his boots clumping noisily on the stairs.

Bergman went over to his wife, who had begun to sob, and patted her on the shoulder. "It's all right, Meriam, all right."

"But you heard what he said; he will leave us to die in the mountains!"

Renoudot said, "I will be there with another man. We will make sure you get through."

He said it bravely, but Bergman could see the man was worried. The Basque, who cared only for his sheep, was their guide. Without him they would perish.

Professor Bergman was a thin man, frail, appearing taller than he really was; the sort of man who looks at home in a library. His full head of hair had turned almost to gray. His eyes were bright; alertness tinged with a fear of the situation.

His wife was shorter and tending to fat. Her face was round but still pretty, with full lips and large oval eyes. She had the look of a matron who had once been beautiful and been told so many times. Her cheeks were puffed from the crying.

The daughter spoke for the first time. "I am not going unless David comes with us." She held her head high, her dark eyes full of tears. She had all the beauty her mother had had in youth and more. She was taller, more graceful. Her long hair was tangled and uncombed, but soft and silky even in disarray. She was a beautiful young woman with finely honed features and an arrogant jaw.

"Who is David?" Renoudot asked.

"The boy . . . the gentleman . . . she is to marry. He was supposed to come here and go with us but . . ."

Bergman's voice trailed off, baffled by the endless possibilities that prevented the young man from being where he was supposed to be. In these times it was foolish to speculate on the whereabouts of anyone because people, especially Jews, disappeared by the thousands, and it was impossible to find out where they had gone and often dangerous to inquire.

"I will not go unless he goes with us."

"But you must go," Renoudot said. "The woman who owns this place will throw you out in another day, and the Basque shepherd will not wait. If you stay here, you are endangering everyone's life."

"The others can go. I will wait alone."

"Not here. The woman who owns this place will not allow it because she is afraid."

"I must! I must wait for David." Her eyes darted back and forth frantically. "The woman will let me stay because I am young and pretty, and I will work here if I have to!" She threw herself down on the bed and began to cry.

"Leah!" her mother said, shocked by the suggestion.

Bergman held up his hand, nodding at Renoudot to indicate everything would be all right. The girl was excited. She would calm down, and when it was time, she would go.

The Frenchman patted him on the arm. "Tomorrow afternoon. Be ready."

After he was gone, Bergman returned to his chair and

looked at the sobbing figure on the mattress. Leah was twenty-three years old and headstrong. She would be determined to remain, but when the time of departure came, she would break down and go with her family. Never argue with the children. Let them alone and they will do the right thing. They were good children, and he loved them.

The son, Samuel, limped over to another mattress. A strange boy, his father thought. Quiet and introspective, forever brooding over something. He will be all the things a man wants of an only son, all of them.

If he lives.

We have come to that. A primitive struggle to keep flesh on bone. A struggle we have ignored because our way has not been the way of the flesh but of the soul.

What good is all of it? This *is* a world of the flesh. I am persecuted and driven because I am a Jew, and what is a Jew to the persecutors but a piece of unacceptable flesh to be devoured in the flames.

In death we are the perfume of their hearths.

"*Adonoi, Adonoi,*" he said aloud, and his wife looked up questioningly. He glanced at her and smiled.

"Nothing. I was only thinking how little time changes. Jews flee into the mountains whether Rameses sits on the throne of Egypt or Hitler on the throne of Europe."

The woman shuddered at the mention of the German's name. She remembered the first time she had heard it, years ago, and everyone had laughed and said he was a foolish Bavarian. Even then she had shuddered because whenever a Jew hater arose, there were many who cheered him on.

Bergman understood her attitude. He had been a professor of philosophy at the University of Paris, a worldly man accepted in intellectual circles. His books had been published in many languages, and he had something of a reputation as one of the intellectual leaders opposed to the hatred that was seeping out of Germany. He had written a defense of Herschel Grynszpan, the distracted youth who shot the first secretary of the German Embassy in Paris on November 6, 1938. He had also mocked the crazy genetic theories proposed by the Nazis, lampooning the foolish doctrines of the Reichsführer, Heinrich Himmler.

His writings made him a favorite among those who claimed war was inevitable and that the French should prepare for it. These men, who formed the nucleus of the future Resistance, became his friends. He gave speeches at their meetings, signed his name on their petitions, and shared his dinner table with them. While they collected rifles and bullets for the coming storm, he put their ideas and philosophy into words.

In the end, of course, his warnings proved to be correct.

On May 10 the Germans smashed into France, overran the surprised Belgians, and for all practical purposes the war was over in a week. The fighting went on for a time, but it was a case of the Germans advancing and the French staggering back. The French army had used outdated tactics by scattering their divisions and their men along the length of the Maginot Line. The Germans massed their tanks into fast-moving Panzer divisions and, together with dive bombers and fighter planes, easily destroyed all opposition as they rolled into the land of their ancient enemy. They also caught the French off guard by going around the Maginot Line and coming through the open door of Belgium. These were the new tactics of armor developed by Fuller, Guderian, and, ironically, De Gaulle. The juggernaut kept going until it smothered Paris.

When Paris fell, and the world fell, Bergman was high on the list of wanted persons. His friends in the Resistance smuggled the professor and his family out of the big house. With little more than the clothes on their backs, they went from hovel to hovel, fleeing in the backs of trucks at night, spending days cooped up in stifling rooms, eating whatever was available, sometimes what could only be described as slop. In slow and painful stages they had moved south, finally to this attic room in a Toulouse bordello.

In a way it was better to be out of Paris and not able to see the terrible humiliation of that proud city. The French flag disappeared and was legally displayed in only one single place—in a locked glass cabinet at the army museum of Les Invalides. In its place thousands of black, white, and red swastikas fluttered in the gloomy air.

The Germans comandeered buildings, set up sentry boxes and checkpoints, stole the city's bronze statuary and shipped it back to Germany, instituted curfews, took over the hotels, shot hostages, and in general let the French know they were a conquered people. In the eyes of most Frenchmen the greatest degradation of all was the daily march of 250 soldiers down the Champs-Elysées to the Place de la Concorde, led by a brass band playing the booming notes of "Preussens Glorie"—Prussia's Glory.

The Resistance fought back from the beginning. It was difficult. They had not only the Germans to contend with but also the French collaborators. These traitors helped the Germans put together lists of wanted men and then helped make the arrests. The men of the Resistance worked equally hard to get these men like Professor Bergman to safety.

The road to safety was very difficult.

*   *   *

Bergman pitied his wife, who had never had any but the easiest of lives. She had been born into a wealthy merchant family and could not conceive of a home without servants. Her father had been a banker, the son of a banker, the grandson of a needle-and-thread peddler who had turned to coin selling, building his fortune into the bank that bore his name. Not an empire like the Rothschilds', or anything like that, but a substantial business all the same.

But the day they actually left Paris, Meriam had surprised him. To all her relatives who still believed themselves safe and the Bergmans foolish to flee, she said, "God has chosen me as Isaac's wife, and a wife obeys God by obeying her husband." She was calm about all of it. To see her during the last month was a burden on his heart, but he was surprised how little she complained.

She is more Jewish than I, he thought. A simple woman who accepted her religion and never stopped to worry about it, while I have spent my life pursuing the intellectual beliefs of everyone and now, with an emotional crisis on my hands, find myself without any real belief to sustain me.

His wife had not gone through life questioning anything and everything. What she was told, she believed.

And what of myself? I do not believe. I have no faith. I am a dry, argumentative, desiccated textbook.

I am dust.

He felt his arm. It was thin, puny. He knew his legs were the same. He had never paid any attention to his body except to see that he did not eat too much and grow fat.

And now, thinking of the trip ahead, he was afraid. The mountains were high and cold. The Basque guide would desert them if they could not keep up. They would try, but the only one he was certain of was his daughter. She was tall and slender and an excellent swimmer. She could keep up with the Basque, but if the others could not, would she go on and leave her family? No, he thought sadly, no more than she will leave us tomorrow and wait for David. She will stay with her family, and if they die, she will die with them.

It was such a senseless death.

His daughter always took his breath away. She was so beautiful and sure of herself. A prize, his friends said, and their sons looked at her with desire.

He was proud that his seed could carry such beauty. The long, straight black hair, the wide eyes, the smooth forehead, signifying intelligence and strength of will; all of it had sprung from his own flesh, and all of it he loved with his whole soul. Nothing was too good for Leah. He was jealous of David, the young man she was to marry. David, not he, would grow old with her, love her through the ages of her life, rest in peace at her side through eternity.

Bergman suddenly realized his son was staring at him. He went over and sat on the edge of the cot. "Don't worry, my son. Everything is going to be all right."

The boy said nothing.

"You will see," Bergman continued. "Soon it will be like the old days, and we'll be sitting in front of a fire, telling stories."

The son said nothing.

He chuckled. "I can even think of one now," Bergman said. "This place we are in, Toulouse, used to be called Tolosa, the capital of the Tectosages, a place famous for its treasure of gold and silver. The Romans lusted after the treasure, and they sent the consul, Quintus Cervilius Caepio, to get it. The Tectosages hid their treasure in the bottom of a nearby lake, and Quintus tortured the unfortunate inhabitants until he learned of the gold's hiding place.

"He drained the lake and recovered the treasure, but it didn't last long because someone assassinated Quintus. The Romans came back and almost exterminated the entire Tectosage nation.

"What do you think of that, my son?"

The son, Samuel, had been staring at his father throughout the entire monologue. There was a short, uncomfortable silence before the boy spoke.

"Are you afraid of the mountains?"

Bergman cleared his throat. "The mountains? Well, they're not going to be easy, but we'll get through," he said with a cheerfulness he did not really feel. "Besides, we have that guide to help us."

Samuel looked straight into his father's eyes. "And what will you do when the guide leaves us?"

Bergman looked at his son and then looked away. There were tears in his eyes, the tears of a father who, for the first time in his life, had no answers for his son.

He patted the boy on the shoulder and indicated he should lie down and sleep. As the boy let his body drop back on the cot, Bergman walked to the door and stared at the wall.

How little equipped I am to handle this situation, he thought. How little I know about the real world, the one that exists outside the world of books. Here it is with everything going to pieces, my children living in filth, and I do not have any idea of what to do to save us.

He decided to go to sleep. Better to sleep than to stay awake and count the knots in the heart.

*   *   *

It was very late at night in the dingy police station. Several gendarmes loafed to one side, eating pieces of bread and cheese and talking in low tones. A few naked light bulbs broke through the gloom, revealing peeling paint on the walls and uncollected dust on the floor. A German Wehrmacht captain sat behind a desk reading a newspaper. Nearby, a German soldier was cleaning his nails with a knife.

The door opened, and everyone's eyes briefly looked up and saw the SS captain entering. It was only a momentary flicker of interest. SS captains were not unusual in police stations.

The SS man looked across the room and saw the Wehrmacht officer. He smiled.

Captain von Berkow was a very handsome man. Tall, slender, graceful. His blond hair and tanned features made him look like one of the "Nordic gods" Hitler was always talking about, an Adonis in uniform, a charter member of the Master Race that was inheriting the earth. His uniform was custom-fitted and carefully pressed. The smooth line of the coat sleeve ended at the tops of the leather gloves, which were folded back, revealing a soft fur lining. His boots were of soft, creaseless oxhide.

He looked down pleasantly at the Wehrmacht officer, who looked up from his newspaper with a bored, official smile.

"Yes, Captain, what may we do for you?"

Captain von Berkow said nothing, only reached inside his jacket and pulled out a sheaf of several papers. He placed them on the desk in front of the officer.

The Wehrmacht man sighed and picked up the papers. He read for about fifteen seconds, and then his eyes widened at the contents. He leapt up from the chair and threw out his arm in a stiff Nazi salute. "Heil Hitler!"

he bellowed, causing everyone in the room to jump to attention.

Von Berkow raised his arm halfway up in a salute, a sardonic expression on his face.

"I am looking for a man."

3

It was late afternoon.

Alain Renoudot sat in the café and watched Professor Bergman and his son enter and take a table at the other end. In a few minutes they were joined by the wife and daughter.

Other people were scattered around the room, sipping wine from cheap glasses, ignoring everything but their own table and glass. A postman sat in the corner and snored, a half-empty glass of wine before him. No one was well dressed. They all looked tired and shabby, as if they were overwhelmed by the Occupation.

Where was that damned Basque? It was getting late, and they would miss the train and perhaps lose their lives while that disagreeable shepherd made love to a whore.

He had worked himself into a temper by the time the shepherd arrived. "You are late."

The Basque scowled. "I am here."

There was no sense arguing; it was better to get down to business. Renoudot began explaining the route to the train station. As he was finishing, he saw two gendarmes enter the café. They went from table to table checking papers, not really suspicious, only doing a job that was in the day's orders.

Even so, Renoudot started to sweat as the policemen came closer and closer to the Bergman table. The Bergmans' forged papers would not deceive anyone who looked closely. Maybe the police would not look closely. Maybe they were loyal Frenchmen who did this work for appearances but would sell their souls before they helped the Germans. Maybe, and then again, maybe not.

Meriam Bergman saw the police, and her hand reached out and grabbed her husband's arm, resting on the round worn table, her knuckles turning white from the pressure. The Basque looked at the woman and then at the police and finally at Renoudot.

Renoudot's brow was covered with sweat. He was afraid and almost frozen to the spot. It was the girl, Leah, who brought him out of his funk.

"What are you going to do?" she whispered.

The Frenchman looked at her, and at that moment he knew what he had to do. They were in his care. He could not let them be captured if he could do anything to avoid it. He looked at the others and spoke in a whisper.

"Listen to me; I am going to create a disturbance."

"What are you going to do?" the Basque said, his eyes on the police.

"Get them to chase me. As soon as they leave, you take the family to the station."

"And you?"

"I will follow as soon as I lose the police."

He got up from the table, walked a little way, then kicked over a chair. As the gendarmes turned toward the clatter, Renoudot ran for the door.

"Hey, you! Stop!"

He ran into the street, turning away from the train station, racing up a side street.

"Stop! Police! Stop, you!"

It was an easy diversion. As he started to cross another road, a car pulled up and blocked his way. The gendarmes were still shouting for him to stop, and he hesitated, trying to decide which direction to go.

Then a uniformed German stepped out of the car, a pistol in his hand.

For an instant Renoudot wanted to run, but the German was only a few feet away, and he could not miss if he pulled the trigger, so he stopped, faced the German, and put his hands behind his neck. As the gendarmes came to a halt before him, he turned and saw the Basque and the Bergman family hurrying out of the café. The little trick had worked.

When Renoudot ran from the café with the police after him, the Basque stood up and motioned for the Bergmans to follow. When they came outside, he saw that the gendarmes had caught Renoudot at the end of the street. He turned and hurried away, the family scurrying to keep pace with his long strides. The older woman moved with choppy steps, almost a trot, her breath growing shorter and her face turning red.

These people are nothing but trouble.

He could be back in the house with the woman. She was plump and good to touch. He had been with her all night and all day. They had haggled about the price, but he felt rich with all the pesetas and francs in his pocket and had given her almost as much as she wanted.

The Basque walked down the street, filled with regret, the Bergmans close behind.

They came to the *Gare Matabiau*, and Bergman read a chart that directed them toward the train to St. Limoux. It was even more crowded than the night before. Peasants dragging sacks across the train-station floor, the always present, shapeless sacks filled with God knows what being carted about the country. Soldiers with their heavy packs. Everyone pushing and shoving, no more than cattle in transit.

The Basque tensed every time they passed a German in uniform, but there was nothing to worry about. The Germans were busy enough trying to get to their own destinations. Underofficers were swearing; children cried and clutched at their mothers' arms; a bedlam of noise and movement.

The Basque was grateful for the chaos. It allowed the Jews to blend into the crowd. City Jews, he thought, who have spent their lives stealing and cheating, and here I am taking care of them.

He was enraged by the situation. That damned Renoudot, getting himself captured. It was not part of the bargain that he should have to care for these people by himself. Well, he would get them to St. Limoux, and then Perea could take over and pay him the extra four thousand pesetas, or he would leave them on the spot.

A beggar sat at the foot of the wooden steps of the platform. He held out his hand as the group approached, and Bergman reached instinctively into his pocket, then withdrew his hand and looked away when he realized he had no money.

"Worry about yourself, Mister Jew," the Basque said.

He felt better when he saw the man cringe. It wasn't the words—Mister Jew; they didn't mean anything. It was the way they were said, the tone of hate. He had made Bergman feel uncomfortable. Good. These people were making him feel uncomfortable. They should be made to understand they were a great inconvenience, a burden, a heavy chain about his neck.

They climbed aboard the train and found seats. The car was crowded this time, filled with peasants who carried sacks and bags, the wealth of the city going back to their villages and towns.

One man played a harmonica. He had a nervous tic that caused his head to jerk, and this caused him to hit a wrong note. An old woman seated near him smiled and moved her head in time with the music, scowling every time he h.t the wrong note, going back to her smile when the man picked up the tune.

An old man with sunken eyes sat on a bench, his shoulders hunched forward, his chin resting on his hands, which held the top of his cane. Like the others in the car, he wore old, ill-fitting clothes. His coat was threadbare, and there was a rip in the shoulder with a piece of padding sticking out. His fat wife sat beside him, chattering incessantly. The old man paid no attention to her.

This train was even more dilapidated than the one that had brought the Basque to Toulouse. The "seats" were hard wooden benches, unpainted, placed close together. The center aisle was barely two feet across. Several windows were cracked, and the paint was peeling from the walls.

A black-uniformed German came aboard and stood at the end of the car. The harmonica player became silent. Everyone sank in their seats. The German's gaze rested only briefly on the Bergmans. They were poorly dressed, or looked poorly dressed in the dim light, the dust of the streets on their shoulders and faces. They blended into the grayness and dinginess around them. The Basque became very interested in a sausage held by a peasant seated across the aisle.

Finally the German left, and people relaxed.

For the first time the Basque looked closely at the Bergman girl. Her eyes were red and swollen. It was clear she had been crying.

"Why does she cry?" he asked Bergman.

"She does not want to leave."

"Why not?"

"The man she is to marry was supposed to join us, but he never appeared."

"You mean I was supposed to take him, too?"

Bergman shrugged in helpless admission that it was so. *Another favor to be asked, another act of begging, another injustice to accept.*

"Another one!" the Basque said angrily. "Listen, what do you think I am? Four of you are bad enough—but five! Mother of God!"

"I am sorry."

"I do this for money, but I am beginning to think money is not enough."

"Again, I am sorry."

The Basque studied him for a moment. "I have never talked with a Jew. We do not have them in the hills. There was one Jewish family I met in a village. He was a tailor. They were killed during the war when they were having dinner. Someone threw a bomb through the window. I didn't see it, but everyone talked about it."

Bergman nodded. He understood. There was a war, and someone used it as an excuse to kill a Jew. They had been doing that for a long time.

"I don't like Jews. Remember that."

"I thought you said you didn't know any?"

"Yes, but I know about them."

The train jolted, a whistle blew, the conductor shouted, and the train huffed, puffed, and began its way slowly through the yard.

The Basque looked out through the grimy window. Another troop train had stopped, and the soldiers were climbing down, walking around, trying to work out the travel soreness that had settled in their muscles.

At the end of the yard he saw animal pens. One of them was filled with sheep, densely packed shoulder to shoulder, the entire mass shifting in a rippling motion away from the clatter made by the passing train. He wondered about his own sheep. They would be without harm. They had food, water, and the dogs. The wolves would stay away.

The train passed through the yard and began moving past rows of shabby houses, first densely packed, sparser as the train reached the outskirts of the city. It soon was doing forty kilometers an hour.

The passengers settled down for the trip. They ate their food—wedges of cheese, bread, and smoked sausages—drank their wine from goatskins, bottles, and jars, and the talk died down. It was night, and they were strongly ruled by their ancestors, a hundred generations of peasants who woke with the sun and went to sleep when it was gone. They leaned back against the seats, finding sleep quickly.

The Basque slouched down and was about to pull the beret over his eyes when he noticed Bergman settling in his seat. He looked at the man for a few moments and then at Meriam, who was sitting between her husband and the shepherd.

"Why is he important?" the Basque asked Meriam.

The woman was surprised. It was the first time the

man had spoken to her. She was afraid of this rough-spoken Basque.

"What do you mean?"

"Many men have gone to a great deal of trouble to help him. Why is he important?"

Meriam nodded her head. "My husband was at the university, a very respected man. I suppose he is important; I don't know. He was always very outspoken."

"About what?"

"The Nazis. He wrote about them. He joined the men who said they would attack France. He told the truth. The Nazis don't like that."

The Basque took another look at Bergman. He might be important, the Basque thought, but he certainly didn't look it.

He shrugged, pulled the beret over his eyes, and settled back to sleep. Meriam stared at him, at his broad shoulders, his hard body, which radiated an animal vitality even in sleep.

The train clattered into the night.

The gendarmes had taken Renoudot to the station house. He had sworn he had not been running away, only trying to catch a friend. There had been much conversation between the arresting officers while the sergeant behind the desk made a number of phone calls. They had argued. Finally, when he thought they were about to release him, they took him to the basement and put him in a cell.

The door clanked shut, and he was left alone. No, not quite alone. He could hear a constant moaning down the hall. Renoudot shuddered, wondering if the man had been beaten.

He looked at his new surroundings. It was a large cell

with several benches. A heavy table, made of planks, occupied the center of the room. The walls were stone; damp, mottled, mildewed stone. The only access was the barred door.

He walked over to the planked table. There were leather straps attached to it. He took one of the straps in his hand and turned it over. It was soiled and stained, a well-used piece of equipment. He suddenly dropped it as he realized what this strap had done; the horrors and injustices it had seen, been a part of.

What am I worried about? he asked himself. What can they do? I have papers, and running is no crime. I was doing nothing wrong. It is nothing. Eventually they will believe my explanation because they have no reason not to believe it. But he was terrified it might not go so easily. All his life he had lived in fear of one thing.

How could anyone stand to be hurt?

The idea of pain haunted him. Pain was a living thing for the boy who hated sports because it was easy to get hurt, but he had forced himself to play football, to run up and down the field kicking the ball, blocking with his body, taking chances. He played well and was able to keep his fear to himself. His father owned a bake shop and displayed the medals won by his son.

"Yes, yes," he would say, "these medals were won by my son. A good athlete, very good, the best. Absolutely fearless, that boy, fearless."

His father was a great one for courage and spoke about the great war and how his son was the right age for the next one. "The life of a soldier is hard, but it is good training for a young man. It teaches him discipline. It makes him hard, better able to cope with life."

He had gone on and on, telling his son about the glories of soldiering, speaking of army movements and battles as if he knew about such matters when in truth he had never been a front-line soldier, only a cook, who had never been in battle.

As the boy grew older, he noticed his father's part in the war grew larger through the telling. What had once been a skirmish was now a battle; what had been a squad action was now the movement of a battalion. It was the same with all the other men who told stories and whose youth grew braver and more adventurous as they grew older and more sedate. As they became more bored with tending bake shops or wine shops, selling meat, cutting cloth, wasting their days on the counting of francs and centimes, they thought back with growing fondness to the days when they had trimmer bellies and clearer eyes.

But Alain Renoudot grew up dreading the thought of war. It was one thing to force himself to play games, another to face guns. He wasn't afraid of death. Death would be easy. One moment you are, the next you are not. What he feared was being shot and lying in pain.

In the end there had been no opportunity to join the army. France had collapsed almost at once before the onslaught of the Germans. Afterward Renoudot had forced himself to follow his friends who joined the Resistance. There he had kept his fears to himself, but now, pacing the narrow cell, he was afraid he would have to face the truth: *He was a coward.* It was a fact he had never admitted, not even to himself. But that was what he was. Playing sports, joining the Resistance, working against the Nazis were things he had forced himself to do in order to hide the truth.

He heard footsteps in the corridor. Heavy, certain steps from booted feet. They stopped in front of his cell. The door opened.

A German captain in a black uniform entered. Renoudot looked up at him. The German smiled.

It was Captain Gunther von Berkow.

He smiled again, showing two straight lines of white teeth. Renoudot smiled back, and then, remembering his intention of acting stupid, he let his head hang down.

"It appears you have gotten yourself into a bit of a mess," the German said. He spoke French easily, although his accent was heavy, and he had a tendency to hang on his "s" sounds and drag them out in a slight hiss.

The Frenchman looked up. "A mistake, I assure you. This is all a mistake."

The German tapped his boot with a leather riding crop.

"What are you doing in Toulouse?"

Renoudot had prepared his story long ago, a plausible story with witnesses to back it up. "I am a baker from a small town. It is difficult to make a living there. I have been thinking of buying a shop here. There are several for sale."

The German was still smiling. "Do you know how to make good German coffee cake? The kind with brown crumbs?"

"Yes, but you should try my pastries. My father taught me to make the best pastries in France, better than any you can get in Paris."

"I would like to try them."

Renoudot relaxed. This was not going to be difficult. The German was friendly, not at all suspicious.

"I have been looking at your papers. Your name is Alain Renoudot, and you are a baker, as you say, but there is one important paper which is missing."

Renoudot looked at him in surprise.

"Think about it."

Renoudot said nothing.

"You know which paper I am talking about."

"No."

"The one that says you belong to the Resistance group

of saboteurs and spies. The one that says your job is to smuggle wanted men out of France."

Renoudot felt a tingle go through his body, making him dizzy. There seemed to be no blood in his hands.

He looked at the German, who said nothing.

"I do not know what you . . . I am only a baker . . . a poor man who . . ." His voice trailed off.

"Of course you are. What do we Germans know? After all, who are we? Stupid northerners. Easy prey for you clever French. That is why we are the masters, and you the servants."

"But this time you *are* making a mistake, I assure you. I have never been a member of the Resistance. I have never smuggled people out of France."

The German clicked his tongue against the roof of his mouth. "Well, in that case, it is possible we have made a mistake. Do you think the SS can make a mistake?"

"We are all human, Captain," Renoudot answered as pleasantly as possible. He did not like to suggest the Germans made mistakes, but in this case there was no other answer.

"I agree. It is possible for the SS to make a mistake. However, I am not SS."

Renoudot was puzzled.

"I am SD. We do not make mistakes."

The Frenchman shivered again. The SD, the dreaded *sicherheitsdienst*, the secret police of the SS, the most feared of all the Nazis, men reported to have unlimited power and who were supposedly responsible only to Himmler himself.

"You can appreciate how painful it is for me to point all this out because I know you had hopes of deceiving everyone and convincing them you were only a harmless baker."

He clicked his tongue again. "That is one of the purposes of the SD. To make people more truthful, to keep them from deceiving themselves."

Renoudot was uncertain how to behave. The captain was amusing himself, playing with him the way a cat teases a mouse.

"I have never smuggled people out of France."

"And Reichsmarschall Goering does not like to eat," the captain said sarcastically. He walked across the cell and stood, his back toward the prisoner. Finally he turned around.

"Where is Professor Bergman?"

4

The Basque had fallen asleep. Borgman and his son and daughter also slept. Only Meriam remained awake, her eyes going from her son to her daughter and, occasionally, to the face of the shepherd. But even she was beginning to feel heavy-lidded. The monotonous clack-clacking of the wheels over the ties was a very peaceful sound.

And then a terrific explosion rent the air.

The train rocked, slamming car into car, tumbling people out of their seats as the wheels left the tracks. There was an awful grinding and screeching of metal, and then the train stopped, settling down in a cloud of dust. There was a fire up by the engine, and great clouds of steam billowed against the black sky.

The Basque had been knocked to the floor but was unhurt. He peered out the window and saw that the passenger car had been jolted in a way that made the front truck come off the rails. The car was bent at an angle that allowed him to see forward toward the engine. The locomotive had been blown apart. At first he suspected the old boiler had burst its seams and exploded in a flash of steam, but then he heard the peasants whispering. *Resistance . . . Resistance.*

It was a scene of chaos.

The train had lurched from side to side, tossing the people about like so many sacks of wheat, slamming them, bruising them, rendering them senseless. Women and men screamed hysterically, fighting to get past one another, going in opposite directions, not really knowing where they were going, moving out of panic and terror.

Two men who were trying to pass one another began fighting, throwing punches, snarling like animals. They fell on top of the old man with the sunken eyes. He tried to defend himself with his cane but was buried under the burly bodies of the other two.

A woman screamed when she saw the blood streaming from her arm, cut by a shard of flying glass.

A child was crying.

Packages, suitcases, boxes, bits of broken benches, glass, debris, unconscious people, littered the floor, and on top of all of it people were screaming and shoving and trying to get off the train.

The Basque looked over and saw Bergman helping his wife to her feet. The girl, Leah, was pulling herself from under a peasant's bundle that had fallen on her. Samuel Bergman was pinned under a seat. The Basque stepped over and pulled the seat, wrenching it from its moorings, freeing the boy. The boy looked at the man but said nothing.

The Basque motioned to the Bergmans to follow and began to make his way through the chaos. He had to climb over the body of the harmonica player, who lay across the aisle, his head tilted at a crazy angle, a pool of blood forming. The neck was bent in a way a neck should not bend. The harmonica lay on the floor a few feet away.

The Basque came to the door, which was blocked by a hysterical man who was pounding on the door and shouting. The shepherd studied the situation for a moment and then reached out and grabbed the man's shoulder. The pressure on his arm made the man turn around.

With a look of contempt for the man, the Basque reached past him and unlocked the door. He gave it a gentle push, and it swung outward. The man who had been hysterical now had a foolish look on his face as the Basque stepped past him and went outside.

The Bergmans followed their guide outside, and they all made their way forward, where the Basque looked at the engine. He realized it was beyond repair for this night at the least. The blazing coals had poured out the side of the wounded engine, spreading out, scorching the grasses and weeds. There was a mangled body near the rear of the engine. It was the engineer, or most of the engineer. He was missing a leg and part of his face. The fireman was on the ground a little distance away, moaning and rocking his leg back and forth. He moaned too loudly and moved the leg too quickly to be very hurt. Somewhere in the night a dog barked.

Bergman and the Basque stood together, watching the people mill about, whispering, wondering what to do.

"Who did this?" the Basque asked.

"The Resistance," Bergman said.

"Who?"

."Frenchmen who fight the Germans."

The Basque was perplexed. "But there were no Germans on this train."

Bergman shrugged.

"They blow up French trains for France?" the Basque persisted.

"Yes."

The Basque shook his head. "They are crazy."

"They are French," Bergman said.

The Basque thought about the situation. The engine was destroyed, the train was off the tracks, and the passengers could do nothing but wait until help arrived. That might not be until morning. After the train became overdue in St. Limoux, the wireless operator would call Toulouse, and Toulouse would tell them it had departed. After more waiting, St. Limoux would wire back that the train had not arrived. They would trace it, eventually find it, and send help.

The shepherd realized it was too dangerous for the Bergmans to wait. The Germans would come to see what had happened and would be angry and suspicious of everyone. They would inspect papers, and the faces of the Bergmans, pasty-faced from city living, would be singled out from the crowd of sun-darkened peasants.

They had to get away.

The Basque touched Bergman on the arm and pointed to a narrow dirt road that ran alongside the railway tracks. The professor understood and motioned for the rest of his family to follow. No one saw them leave.

The Basque walked with long strides, and the others did their best to keep up. For two hundred meters the road went parallel with the tracks, but then it turned away from the tracks and went off between the fields. It was flat, rolling country, fenced off to mark the fields. Trees lined the road.

Look at them, the Basque thought.

The boy took three steps to match two of his own, and the mother was already pressing her side as if in pain. She was wearing expensive, thin-soled shoes that were better suited to walking on thick carpets than on rocky slopes. *She will walk and stumble until she falls and cannot go on, and then I will leave her.*

He wanted to leave them now, but his bargain with Perea and Renoudot had been to get these people to St. Limoux and into the mountains. That was the bargain, and he would keep his part. Their part of the bargain was to match his pace, and if they could not, it was their problem.

As the Basque strode down the road, bathed in a silver shower of moonlight, he suddenly stopped and listened. In the distance he heard the sound of an approaching siren. It was coming quickly. The Basque turned and signaled for the others to get off the road.

Everyone froze as the siren drew closer and then was abreast of them on the road. It was a German staff car speeding in the direction of the train wreck. When the car was gone, the Basque led them back onto the road, and they continued away from the area of the train wreck.

They passed alongside a dilapidated wooden fence. In the distance the Basque could see a farmhouse with an old barn standing between the road and the house. He held up his hand. While the others waited, he climbed through the fence and went into the barn.

There were animals in stalls, and he decided it would be wise to spend the night there. It was cold on the road, and he did not know where he was going in the dark.

A horse snorted and stamped a foot.

The cows grumbled in their sleep.

The chickens were in their coop, asleep and unaware.

The Basque had anticipated a dog and was happily surprised when none appeared. The farmer probably had an old pet who was spending his twilight years sleeping in the house.

He came back outside and looked at the farmer's home. It was an ordinary frame house, low on the ground with a steep roof, painted white. The roofing was a darker color, made of thatch or some other natural material. He thought he could see flowers in window planters, but it was too dark to be sure. He was pleased that the house stood a good distance away from the barn.

He motioned for the others to join him, cautioning them to silence by bringing his forefinger to his lips.

The five entered the barn and with the help of the faint moonlight felt their way to a rough-hewn ladder leading to a hayloft. The Basque climbed up and watched as the others clumsily followed him.

The Bergmans were soon asleep. Except Leah. She sat with her back against a post, her eyes staring at nothing in particular until she noticed another pair of eyes.

It was the Basque.

Leah gazed back and held his stare. And then her lids drooped, and she was asleep.

Captain von Berkow's question about Professor Bergman shocked Renoudot. There had been a long silence, the SD man watching his prisoner closely.

"Before you protest that you know nothing about Professor Bergman, let me tell you about him," the German said, walking over to the hard bench. "May I sit down?"

Renoudot nodded. What a strange SD man, smiling and asking permission from a prisoner to sit.

"The good professor is not just anyone," the German said. "He has quite a reputation as a philosopher, scholar, and historian. And, of course, he is well known because of his writing. Tch-tch, these scholars, they never leave well enough alone. Bergman was one of the worst offenders. He was, in fact, one of the leaders of the Communist-Jewish front. The Reichsführer has him high on the list of people who are dangerous to the new order. Smoke?"

He held out a packet of cigarettes, and the Frenchman took one and allowed the German to light it for him.

"He is a slippery fellow, this Bergman," the captain continued. "Each time we think we have him, we always find ourselves one step too late. It seems he has many friends who wish to get him out of the country. The international Jewish plot, no doubt."

He looked carefully at Renoudot. "Why do you let them do this to you? Don't you people ever learn?"

"Them? Do what?"

"You aren't Jewish. Why do you let the Jews trick you into doing their work?" He shook his head. "They fool everyone. The only people who understand them and are dealing with the problem are the Germans. The French have looked the other way while their country has been corrupted by Jews.

"But what's done is done, and now we must catch Bergman, and you know where he is."

"I don't know anything about this."

"My friend, you misunderstand. I don't wish to make this a troublesome experience. There is no sense making denials. I know who you are and what you are doing here because one of your own people is an informer."

Renoudot began to perspire. Who could the informer be? How much did this German really know?

"Our informer tells us that your plan was to take Bergman out of France. I don't quite understand how you proposed to do that, but it is unimportant.

"I've been doing a little thinking. My informer says you are an intelligent man. Such a man does not jump up and run out of a café without reason.

"I think Bergman was in the café when the gendarmes began checking papers. You ran out to lure them away. It almost worked. The French police thought it was only a foolish incident and would have released you. Fortunately, they had the good sense to tell us about it, and your description matched the one given us by the informer."

He looked at the prisoner with an expression of compassion. "Yes, that informer again. Quite a useful man from our point of view. Now, won't you tell me where Bergman is hiding and get this over with?"

Renoudot thought quickly. If Mercier or Breveulette or Perea had been the informer, the captain would already be in St. Limoux. But he was not. Therefore, it was safe to assume the traitor was someone on the fringe of the group, someone with a very limited knowledge.

It was a question of time. When Perea learned of the incident in the café and his arrest, he would immediately take the others into the mountains.

I can save Bergman. It is only a matter of stalling for time.

Renoudot was surprised to learn that Bergman was an important person. He had not suspected it from the looks of the man, and no one had told him that the Nazis considered him dangerous. Well, this was the way things were in the Resistance. No one was told anything he did not need to know. The less a man knew, the less he could be forced to tell. It was a good system. If he had known that Bergman was important, he would have been more nervous, and a nervous man makes more mistakes. Perhaps he could gain time for Bergman by pretending to admit to some things but really not telling anything.

"Very well. I am a member of the Resistance."

The SD captain smiled.

"I was here to help Bergman escape. And what you said about the café is true. Bergman was there. I was to arrange a contact with a man who would take them. . . ."

"Them?"

Damn! The German hadn't known about the family. He should not have told him, but it slipped out, and it was too late, so better to keep going and sound honest.

"The Bergman family."

"How many in the family?"

"A wife and two children. Boy and girl."

"Ages?"

"The girl about twenty. The boy, maybe fifteen."

"Good."

"The contact was to take them east to the Gulf of Lions where a boat would pick them up. But the police came, and I ran out of the café to distract them, as you have already guessed. I don't know what happened after that. I assume Bergman made contact with the next agent."

"A very plausible story. You are only the middle man. Someone else takes Bergman to the coast where yet another man is waiting to drive the boat. Yes, yes, quite plausible. Tell me, where is the boat taking him?"

"I'm not sure. Someplace in Africa, I think."

The German sat, brooding over what had been said, and Renoudot began to think his deception had worked. Then the captain looked at him and said, "Do you know what we do to someone from the Resistance when we catch him?"

There was a moment of silence.

"We shoot him. But there are times when shooting is an act of mercy. Sometimes a man begs to be shot."

He stood up quickly and crashed his riding crop across the side of Renoudot's face.

The pain was intense, and Renoudot touched the ugly red line with his hand. *It was beginning.* It was going to happen. The thing he dreaded.

He felt the liquid run down his leg. Warm, saline. A puddle formed beside his shoe.

The German saw it and smiled.

5

_____

The barn was warm. There was a dampness. The sweet smell of hay. Crackling noises.

The movement of hoofs.

The barn groaned as the new warmth seeped into its old wooden bones.

The Basque looked at the Bergmans and saw they were asleep, except the boy, who was thoughtfully chewing on a piece of hay.

The light of the new day came through the cracks in the barn walls, and the Basque decided they had better be up and on their way.

"Boy," he said, and Samuel dropped the hay and looked up.

"Wake the others."

Samuel stood up, bits of hay and straw sticking to his clothes. He shook his mother and father on the shoulders. The woman was instantly awake, but Bergman came slowly from sleep, resisting the beginning of another day.

The Basque came down the ladder and stopped to admire the horses. They were draft animals with hoofs the size of platters and rippling shoulder muscles that glistened in the dim light. One of them grunted in the pleasure of sleep.

It was chilly outside, and the clear air instantly erased the contented feeling the Basque had enjoyed in the animal warmth of the barn.

Bergman came out and rubbed his arms. "Cold, isn't it?"

"The mountains are much colder."

"Yes, yes, I suppose they are.."

They turned to see a farmer coming toward them. He had a heavy stick in his hand. He was a big man, as big as the Basque. He wore a green shirt under a stained blue sweater. His beaked nose came out of a field of flesh that was furrowed with lines. A scar broke the smoothness of his chin. His mouth was twisted in a snarl, a very unfriendly sight; his manner was menacing.

"Who are you? What are you doing here?"

The shepherd looked at the man, noting the beret, the *makhila* in his hand, the trace of Basque enunciation in his French.

"We have spent the night in your barn," the Basque replied, using the tongue common to them both.

The farmer lowered his *makhila* the moment he heard the beloved language.

"We needed shelter and used your barn. We have disturbed nothing, hurt nothing."

"Were you comfortable?" the farmer asked the group.

The Basque held up his hand. "They can't understand you. Only me."

The farmer looked at Bergman. "Who is this one?"

"A Jew. I am being paid to take them to St. Limoux."

The farmer nodded. Crazy things happened since the Germans came, and men were forced to do strange work. Even Basques.

"Does this road go to St. Limoux?"

"No, not this road. You take this one until you come to the crossroads at Magalan. Then go right. That is the road to St. Limoux."

The shepherd nodded. "May I buy some food? Bread? Cheese?"

"How much do you want?"

The Basque handed over two coins. The farmer looked at the money and jerked his thumb toward the others. "What about them?"

"If they have money, they can buy food."

The farmer turned to Bergman and spoke in French. "Do you have any money to buy food?"

Bergman shrugged. "No."

The farmer pointed to the well. "The water is free."

He went to the farmhouse, returning swiftly with a half loaf of dark bread, a large hunk of cheese, and a small jar of wine. The Basque ate while the Bergmans watched. Leah said "pig" but her father quieted her. The Basque finally gave the family some scraps.

They left the farmer and continued down the road, the Basque taking long strides that widened the gap between himself and the Bergmans. After a while the Basque turned around and realized he was forty meters ahead of the others. *Those fat whores in Toulouse could get through the mountains more easily,* he thought angrily. These people will never make it. The old woman has no strength. The man has no flesh with no strength.

"You must keep up with me," he said when they came up to him. "We have a long way to go."

The man nodded. He glanced at his wife and then at the Basque as if asking pity for the woman.

The Basque shook his head. "There can be no excuses. We must keep going."

They began to walk again, this time the Basque measuring his steps more slowly, letting the professor's wife set the pace. Eventually they must reach St. Limoux. Eventually his part of the bargain would be finished.

They passed between fields being prepared for winter, and in the distance they could see peasants working with huge cream-colored oxen, their backs covered with long linen cloths to protect them from the sun and the flies. A peasant walked behind with a long goad in his hand. At the end of the day the man would be covered with bits of grit and dust that went down into his pores.

An hour later the woman tripped and fell. Her daughter tried to catch her, but she was too late as Meriam went down heavily.

The Basque glowered at her as she painfully rolled to a sitting position.

"My wife is tired," Bergman said. "Very tired. Perhaps a five-minute rest?"

"A five-minute rest here, a five-minute rest there; soon we will have lost an hour."

"I know it is an inconvenience, but I must ask as a special favor. She is not used to such exercise."

The Basque grunted and sat down on the grass by the side of the road. The others understood he was agreeing to the request.

"Tell me, if you cannot keep going here on a smooth road, how do you expect to climb through the mountains?" he asked.

"We will do our best," Bergman said.

"Instead of a road up there you walk on sharp rocks and fallen trees. There are narrow gorges where you have to dance along a stream. Do you think you can do that?"

"We will do it," the girl said quietly.

"Perhaps you," the Basque said. "But not her." He pointed at Meriam with his stick.

"We will get through."

"Of course."

"We will."

"I will leave you if you have to stop like this in the mountains."

"Then leave."

"We are taking too long. The snow is growing in the clouds."

"We will do what we have to do to make it through."

"There are wolves up there," the Basque said, enjoying himself. "Killers who can knock down a sheep and take out its throat on the run. Their teeth are an inch long, and they move like shadows through the forest."

The mother began crying softly, and Leah walked over to the Basque and stood defiantly in front of him.

"Shut up! It's bad enough without this. Leave her alone."

"I only say the truth."

"Just shut up, damn you, you filthy swine, shut up!"

The Basque smiled and nodded his head. He took out his pipe and filled it with tobacco.

There was movement on the road. The Basque stood up and watched the wagons, leaving a thin wisp of dust in the air behind them. There were three wagons in all, each pulled by a single horse, moving leisurely. Several children and dogs ran alongside, and a couple of goats tied by ropes walked behind each one.

"Who are they?" Bergman asked.

"Nothing to worry about. Gypsies, probably."

For five minutes they watched as the wagons came closer. Finally the first one stopped in front of them. A huge mountain of a man with a triple chin and mounds of creased flesh in the back of the neck was driving. He had a filthy green kerchief tied around his neck and was chewing the stem of an unlit pipe.

The other two wagons stopped behind the first. They were wooden wagons, all painted a garish red, their sides laden with pots, pans, tools, and sacks of food. The curious people looked out from the wagons, and the Basque estimated their number at more than twenty. The women wore colorful dresses, but the men were more blandly dressed in the dark clothing of peasants. Some of them wore bright, colorful caps or kerchiefs, which was unusual.

The Basque looked toward the man driving the first wagon, assuming he was the leader.

The man smiled and spoke.

"Are you in trouble?" It wasn't a voice. A rumble brought up from the bottom of a pit. His entire body, not the mouth alone, seemed to move as he spoke.

"The woman fell. She will be all right," the Basque said. He looked at the wagons and saw the peering faces. He had been correct. A family, or families, or whatever it was they called themselves, of Gypsies.

"Are you going in this direction?" the fat Gypsy asked.

"Yes."

"We have room."

"We have nothing to steal."

The fat Gypsy looked surprised for a second and then burst into peals of laughter that shook the wagon and clattered the pots and pans hanging on its sides.

"From those who have something to steal, we steal. Those who have nothing, we help. Get in the wagon."

The Basque climbed onto the seat next to the Gypsy. The Bergmans helped themselves aboard in the rear. The seat shook as the Gypsy laughed again. It was an old, stale joke, that about stealing. Gypsies were proud of their reputations as thieves. The Basque had made a friend.

They began to move forward, and the children now crowded around the first wagon, intent on getting a better look at the strangers. Their thin, half-starved dogs trotted at their heels, more wary now, ready to flee the kick of a strange boot. They were half wild, these mongrels, descendants of stolen dogs, carelessly interbred and undernourished for generations. Although capable of using their jaws to defend themselves, they had learned it was better to flee trouble than oppose it.

"Where are you going?" the Basque asked as he relit his pipe.

"St. Limoux. This is a good time. We always go there at this time. The peasants have money from their crops. We give a small carnival, and some of the money comes to us."

"We are going to St. Limoux."

"You can go with us. It is more comfortable in a wagon."

"And better for that old woman," the Basque said. "She would not make it on foot."

The Gypsy eyed him carefully. "You are a family?"

"They are a family."

"And you?"

"I am being paid to take them to St. Limoux."

"The pay is much?"

"No, and I have not been paid yet," he lied. "But these are hard times, and a man must take what comes along."

The fat Gypsy cursed. "Hard times is right! Ever since the Germans came, there have been nothing but hard times. People are no longer interested in fun. We put on a little show, and only a few come to see it. Then a German shows up, and even they leave. Besides, the Germans hate Gypsies. I know of a family of Gypsies that disappeared. Disappeared—ha! It was the Germans."

"Were you in Toulouse?"

"God forbid, no! The big cities are filled with Germans. They won't let us camp anywhere. We stay in the country and the villages."

He reached into a sack, took out two small red onions, and handed one to the Basque. They peeled off the outer layers and sat on the creaking seat board, slowly taking bites.

At this time of the day the big room of the inn in St. Limoux was almost empty. There were over twenty tables, but only four or five were occupied. A drunken shepherd sat talking to himself in the corner near the fireplace. He had a bottle of wine in front of him and every few minutes would raise it to his lips and drink, then return to his conversation with himself, punctuating it with violent denunciations every now and then.

Perea sat in the far corner of the café near a small window that gave him a view of the street, a glass of untouched wine in front of him. He had been at the table since early morning, and it was almost noon.

The stationmaster knew nothing about the train. It had left Toulouse but had not arrived at St. Limoux, and the authorities had said absolutely nothing. If m'sieu would keep checking in, the stationmaster would be pleased to tell him what he knew.

The possibilities frightened Perea. Had the Germans stopped the train? Could they have known about Renoudot and Bergman? And what about the shepherd, Urquijo? He was money hungry and undependable. At the first sign of trouble he would probably disappear.

He tried to calm his fears by telling himself that there had been a mechanical breakdown, that the train was being fixed. Soon it would appear, and everything would be all right. In the meantime, he had checked around the town to see if there would be any problems getting out He was happy to discover the Germans had barely touched this out-of-the-way place. There were only five or six soldiers, who spent most of their time sleeping, playing cards, singing and drinking the local wines. They were supposed to patrol the train station, but there were few trains, and since St. Limoux was an unlikely place to find spies and saboteurs, their inspection of arriving passengers was perfunctory.

Perea realized that if Renoudot and the others could get out of the train station, they would have no problem getting into the mountains. The Germans paid absolutely no attention to the paths leading out of town. Their attitude was that no one could find his way through the Pyrenees, and if a man was fool enough to try, he deserved to die of cold, starvation, or wolves.

He left the inn and walked down to the train station. The air had gotten much colder in the past two days. Thank God he and Andres, the local Resistance man, had hidden heavy clothing and food supplies in a cache on the way into the mountains. At least they would not freeze.

The stationmaster sat in a small cramped office at an old worn desk behind the telegraph key, tapping out a message. After a few moments he stopped and laboriously copied down the return, pausing to lick the point of his pencil after every few words. Finally he pushed back his eyeshade and turned to Perea.

"Yes?"

"Any news of the train from Toulouse?"

"The wires are crackling with news."

Perea shifted his weight from one foot to the other. "What are they saying?"

"Sabotage. Partisans blew it up."

"The whole train?"

"Who knows? A lot of damage. The engine is destroyed. The engineer is dead, the fireman badly wounded."

"What about the passengers?"

"I don't know. The reports vary. Some were injured, but how many and who they are, I don't know. Most of them are probably all right, but m'sieu, believe me, I would tell you if I knew, but I don't."

"But most of the passengers are all right?"

"Probably."

"You're sure?"

"No, of course not. Who can be sure?"

"What is going to happen?"

"I don't know that, either. A repair crew has left Toulouse with another engine. Maybe they will fix the train, and it will come here, or maybe they will bring it back to Toulouse. More than likely they will get it off the tracks and bring a new train here."

"And the authorities?"

"Huh, the authorities. It is not the authorities, it is the Germans. They are furious. They are threatening to shoot every partisan they catch."

"Thank you," Perea said, and went back into the street.

This was a nice complication. If the Bergmans did get to St. Limoux, the Germans would be particularly suspicious.

Mierda!

6

The Gypsies made camp when the sun descended below the hills ahead. The women started up their cooking fires, and delicious smells of onions and beans and garlic filled the air.

The activity of the Gypsies began the moment the wagons stopped. The horses were unhitched by the children. The men dropped sideboards from the wagons, and the women attended to the meal. No one seemed in a hurry, yet there was no wasted activity. It was a thing they had done thousands of times.

The camp itself consisted of the three wagons drawn up in a line with tattered canvas awnings pulled out from the sides to create places of shelter. Buckets served as chairs, and trees as backrests. It was a meeting place put together in minutes, capable of being struck in minutes, a place of the transient.

Leah had ridden in the back of the wagon without saying a word but grateful that her mother no longer had to walk. Meriam had sat with her legs straight before her, her back touching the canvas side, pitching forward and backward with every rut in the road.

Now that the Gypsies were busy with dinner, Leah wandered about the camp, looking curiously at the children. The girls had long, matted hair and wore oversize garments that could be loosened and enlarged as they grew. The boys also wore castoffs. Their faces and hands were filthy.

It never occurred to Leah to help with the preparation of the meal, though she saw her mother helping an old crone with no teeth and a vivid red kerchief on her head. They were cleaning beans. It was to be expected, Leah thought. In their own home her mother had always fussed about, cooking and doing all of the baking herself.

She wandered over where the children were feeding and watering the horses. She noticed that when the Gypsies made camp, the children automatically began to do this work, which was obviously their assigned task. Even the dogs sensed the change in their playmates and went over to the trees and slept.

The men sat in front of the fires filling their pipes, rolling cigarettes, and drinking wine. They spoke rarely. It was a time of peace before the meal. The Basque sat by himself a distance from the fire and smoked his pipe.

"Leah, sit down and get some rest," her father said.

"I have been sitting all day in that cart. I need to stretch my legs." Her tone carried a familiar hint of anger.

"In one of your moods, I see."

She walked to the woods, to the edge of a little stream. *Yes, one of my moods.* What is happening to us that we should be happy?

Being with David was happiness. Having David touch your hair and look in your eyes was happiness. But David was not there, and God knows what had happened to him. Even if she had waited in Toulouse, he might not have come. Maybe she was deluding herself. After all, why should David flee from France; no one was after him.

She looked back toward the camp and saw the meal was being served. Hungry despite herself, she went back and stood by the pot until one of the women filled her plate. It was the first food she had eaten in two days other than the scrap of bread and cheese she had gotten from the Basque farmer.

"How quickly a man gets hungry," her father said.

"This is the best food I've ever eaten."

"Shhh, don't let your mother hear."

"Why isn't she eating?"

"She is helping the women. They wait until the men are finished before they eat."

She looked at him with a startled expression. "I was supposed to wait?"

"It doesn't matter. They understand we have different customs."

The fat Gypsy came toward them, moving gracefully for all the bulk.

"I see you are enjoying the food."

"Yes, thank you. We were very hungry."

"And you, girl, I see you were too hungry to wait for the women."

Leah blushed but refused to be cowed. "Yes, I was hungry. But what is wrong with a woman eating with men?"

The fat Gypsy laughed.

"Hey, Alex," he called to a young man who was eating

nearby. "You were right. This girl has a lot of spirit." He laughed again. "Alex is my son," he explained.

"What is this about my spirit?"

"Alex told me you looked like a woman with fire in her blood. He is usually right. Alex is his father's son, a bull." He laughed again and then sighed for the lost days of his youth.

The men finished their meal, and they began to talk about the German Occupation, the price of wine, of everything and nothing, and Leah left them and went to sit by the stream and listen to the gurgle of the water. The sound soothed her and made it easier to face a problem that had been bothering her all day.

The Basque was right about the mountains. Her mother could never make it. Today's march on the road had proved that. If they stayed with her, they might all die, but they could not leave her to die by herself. Many years ago she had gone on a train through a pass in the Pyrenees when the family had taken their holiday in Spain. She had only been a small child, but she still remembered the height and rugged terrain of the mountains. It was madness to expect her mother to make such a journey on foot.

"You are very beautiful," a voice said, and she jumped. It was Alex, the son of the fat Gypsy.

He was as tall as his father, but instead of fat there was only muscle. He had curly black hair that came down over the tops of his ears. His skin was dark, which made his teeth seem even whiter. He was almost handsome, almost but not quite because of his mouth, which seemed mean and cruel even when he smiled, which was all the time.

"You scared me," Leah said.

"What do you do?"

"Nothing."

"I mean back there, where you come from. Do you work?"

"No."

"I do not work, either. Work is for simple minds. The clever live without working."

"That's disgusting."

"You're very pretty."

"That's no business of yours."

"You have nice skin."

She did not answer.

"I am very strong. The girls like me. I am also handsome, am I not? Look at me from the side. See my chin."

Leah turned away.

"Tell me, am I not good-looking? Look at my muscles. I have them all over my body."

"Go away."

"All the girls tell me I have good muscles," he said with a leer.

When she did not answer, he reached out and touched her arm.

"Keep your filthy hands to yourself."

"Ah-ha! Want to play!" He jumped forward, grabbed her arms, and leaned over to kiss her. She pulled back violently, fighting to get loose from his grip, but it was useless. He was very strong.

She relaxed and let herself be gathered up against him. Then as his lips touched hers, she bit him. Her strong white teeth punctured the skin and came together with a click on the inside of his lip. He released her, put a hand to his torn lip, and cursed. Then abruptly he began to laugh.

"You are a wild one, a wild one!"

He made another lunge at her, but she was too quick

and escaped, running back to the camp. She passed the fat Gypsy, and he laughed when he saw her and his son, the blood dribbling down his chin.

She found her father and brother seated by a fire near the wagon.

"Leah!"

Before Bergman could ask for an explanation, Alex came up after her.

"What is going on?" Bergman asked.

"I meant no harm," the Gypsy said. "I was only having some fun. And then this wildcat . . ."

"My daughter, a wildcat? No, sir, my daughter is a gentle person. . . ."

"Gentle! Look what she did to my mouth when I tried to kiss her!" He pointed to the torn lip, and Bergman cringed.

"She did this," the Gypsy said. "She is an animal."

"You should not have tried to kiss her."

"I kiss them all, love them all," he said, reaching his hand toward the girl who pulled back.

"Please, young man, please leave her alone."

Bergman's pleading tone made the Gypsy sneer. What could this weakling do to stop him? He took another step forward.

"Leave her alone," a voice said from behind him.

He turned and saw the Basque shepherd. The young Gypsy carefully looked him over with a practiced eye. The man was big and strong. His large hands held a heavy walking stick tipped with an iron sheath.

Alex quickly decided the girl was not worth it if it meant trouble with this one. He laughed and swaggered away. Even if they had won, he would not give them any satisfaction.

The Basque looked once at Bergman and walked back to his place by the fire

The professor turned to his daughter, but she had already gone inside the wagon. He suddenly felt the eyes of his son, wide-open, cold. He started to speak, but his son turned his head and looked away.

A soft crying came from the wagon.

Leah lay with her head on her mother's lap.

"There, there, everything is all right."

"But I shouldn't have bitten him so hard. I almost tore his lip off, I bit so hard."

"So you bit so hard, what of it? A big lunk like that, he should be ashamed of himself."

"I have too much of a temper."

"Always you had a temper, even when you were a little girl," Meriam said, a light coming into her eyes as she recalled happier days when she had been the focal point of her children's lives. "Poor old Ruth, what that nanny went through! She would come to me when it was time for your nap, and I would make you go to your bed, and then you would be so angry, you would sometimes tear up one of your dolls."

"I am afraid of my temper. When I get angry, I forget everything and . . . and just do things! Someday I will hurt a person."

"A person like this Gypsy? Who cares?"

Her hands lovingly stroked her daughter's forehead.

"Mama . . ."

"Yes."

"I have been thinking. . . ."

"One minute biting like a cat and the next an intellectual like your father."

"No, this is important. I have been thinking about the mountains. Maybe the shepherd is right. Maybe the mountains are too rugged for us to climb."

"When we get to the mountains, we will see how hard they are to climb."

"Do you think you can climb a mountain?"

"Lately I haven't done it, so who knows?"

"Well, what I've been thinking is that maybe you and I should stay in the little town we are going to. Father and Samuel can go ahead with the shepherd, and we can join them later."

"Why should you stay? You are strong and healthy enough to climb a mountain. If poor Samuel with his bad leg can climb, why can't you?"

"But we can't leave you alone."

"Who says I am staying behind. Do you think I want to stay here in this place with all these crazy Nazis?"

"But the mountains are high and, well, things aren't so bad here."

"Not so bad? May our enemies have things this good!"

"I'm worried."

"As things happen, we will take care of them."

"But . . ."

"If I have to climb the mountain, then I will do it because that is what I have to do. Now let's not talk about it anymore. It is foolish."

It was no use. Her mother would not allow any of the family to worry about her. It was all right when she worried but not the other way around.

"Here," she was saying, changing the subject, "here is some nice cheese. I got it from that old woman who was cutting beans with me."

"I thought you said the Gypsies were dirty?"

"The men, some of them. But the old lady is very nice. She is the fat one's mother. She told me she has been living in wagons like these for seventy years. Imagine, seventy years and never having a home of your own! Some people are not as lucky as others."

The girl nibbled on the hard cheese.

A thought came to her. Even if David wanted to come to her, how would he know where to go when she didn't know where she was going herself?

Sleep came slowly.

Gunther von Berkow always smiled. When watching a woman undress, or in the actual act of coupling, or, as now, listening to the screams of the Frenchman, whose testicles were slowly being crushed in the grip of the clamp. He nodded as the watchful SS soldier gave it another twist. Renoudot screamed again, a long and drawn-out cry, ending in the sound of a choking animal.

"An interesting part of the body, the testicles," Captain von Berkow said conversationally. "They are, at one and the same time, the source of the greatest pleasure and the greatest pain."

He raised his hand and motioned the soldier to take off the clamp. As it loosened and was finally removed, the Frenchman sighed and gritted his teeth as the blood rushed back.

"That's a new feeling, isn't it? Another sort of pain. We have many variations on the theme of testicle pain. We can bind them with piano wire to shut off the circulation for an hour or so. When the wire is removed, the blood rushes back, and the pain is excruciating, or so I am told. I have never felt it myself, but perhaps you will do us the favor of undergoing it as an experiment, and then you will be able to relate the experience."

The Frenchman breathed deeply, his eyes closed, his sweating body making the wooden table clammy. He was tied spread-eagle to the four legs. They had been using the clamp only a few minutes, but the intense pain made it seem like days.

He would try to hold out for one second, one second at a time, only that one second and never think about the next, never admit that more pain was coming.

Von Berkow stood up and folded his hands, fingers interlocked, palms outward. He cracked his knuckles. They made clean, distinct sounds that rippled one after the other.

"Now I think it is time to tell me about Professor Bergman. I don't see that you are having any fun with our little game." He walked over to the table and undid the buckles on the straps that held the Frenchman to the table.

"Sit up and rest a moment. Contemplation is good at a time like this. You have had a taste of how bad it can get. Believe me, it can get worse." He held out a packet of cigarettes. The Frenchman took one in his hands and held it between his lips as the captain lit it with his gold lighter.

The two SS soldiers stood to the side waiting for further instructions. They were thick-set, hardened men in black uniforms who paid no attention to the talk that was going on. In fact, they had shown no particular interest in the torture. It was only another job.

The captain looked thoughtfully at his victim. "Our informer said you were not a brave man. After this," he said, indicating the torture table, "I must disagree. You are brave. Very brave."

Renoudot brought the cigarette to his lips and took a puff. Surprisingly his hands shook less than before the torture started. There was a glaze over his eyes, a sense of being somewhere else, someplace far away. "They say I am a coward," he said to no one in particular. "Yes . . . I have always been a coward . . . as a boy I hated the ball . . . when you had the ball, they came after you. . . ." He stopped as his mind wandered, and he took another puff of the cigarette.

The captain shook his head. "This being a coward is all in your mind, a fantasy." He looked away as if he were thinking of something else. "Why is it we indulge in fantasies which are so far from the truth. In my family's house there is a huge painting of my great-grandfather, *Helmut Christian* von Berkow. It is very handsome. It shows Helmut Christian astride a magnificent white stallion. The horse is rearing, the sword is raised, the man is ready for battle—very brave, very courageous, and . . . very much a lie."

The captain had a wry expression on his face. "Helmut Christian, you see, was a cripple who never rode a horse in his life. The painting was his fantasy."

Renoudot spoke again as if the captain had not said a word. "They would kick the ball to me . . . I hated it . . . but my father was watching . . . an old soldier . . . bravery was important to him . . . a brave son, he called me. . . . Once, when I broke a bone, and they carried me off the field, my father was proud and called me brave."

Von Berkow had been listening but in an abstract way. Something that Renoudot said had triggered his own mind. When he spoke, he really wasn't speaking to the Frenchman but to himself.

"I am supposed to become a general. In my family the men are always colonels and generals, the regular army, the Wehrmacht." He paused, and his tone became more angry. "My own father looks down on me because he does not understand the new order. He looks down on me because he is a Prussian nobleman, and I wear a black uniform. He does not understand that I am part of the new empire."

He had become very angry. "He does not understand

that I am part of the new order and that we must build in ten years what will last a thousand!"

Von Berkow suddenly realized what he was saying, and his anger faded. He relaxed and smiled at the Frenchman.

Renoudot had been watching and listening to the German, and now there was something approaching *understanding* on his face.

Von Berkow saw this look, and whatever humanity had come out in him disappeared. His eyes no longer had sparks in them. They were, once again, dead, bottomless wells; windows without pity. "We are wasting time."

Renoudot looked at him, and for the first time he smiled.

The German looked annoyed.

"This is not the time to learn to be brave."

7

─ ─

The train arrived.

The authorities had brought a second locomotive and string of cars from Toulouse. Out of the train poured the passengers. Perea searched through the crowd. Some were wounded and left neglected on stretchers because the authorities were too busy trying to find out about the sabotage.

Perea could not find Renoudot or the Basque or the Bergman family. He feared to talk to anyone else because the Germans were everywhere, asking questions, dragging off protesting peasants to the church, which had been converted into a prison.

Suddenly a voice at his shoulder made him jump. "Who are you?"

"What!"

"Are you one of the passengers?" the man asked. He

was a French policeman, a *political* in a black leather coat.

"No. I am just a farmer."

"What are you doing here?"

"Everyone talks of the train. I came to see for myself."

The policeman became disinterested. "It would be better for you to go home."

"Yes, of course. Forgive me, I was only curious."

The policeman smiled. "People are all alike. A disaster occurs, and they flock to see it. Everyone enjoys death as long as it is happening to someone else. Cigarette," he offered, holding out a package.

Perea was terrified, but also anxious to take advantage of this sudden intimacy. The policeman had stopped being a policeman for a moment. "Why was the train blown up?" he asked, trying to act nonchalant, puffing on his cigarette.

"Who knows?" the man said with a shrug. "Foolish men do foolish things. But we will catch them. We always do."

"It couldn't have been an accident?"

The policeman looked at him more closely. "Perhaps. Accidents do happen. Our engineers are going through the wreckage. They will determine the cause of the explosion."

Perea hunched over. "Perhaps normal times will return. That will be good."

There was a sudden commotion among the passengers, and two Wehrmacht soldiers emerged from the crowd, dragging a man between them. He began to protest, but one of his captors hit him with the butt of a rifle.

"What is it?" called the policeman who was talking with Perea.

"This man tried to run away. Maybe he is from the Underground."

"Ahhh, now we are getting somewhere," the policeman said, throwing his cigarette to the ground and stomping on it with his foot. "The Underground, eh? So, my friend, this was probably not an accident, after all." He followed the soldiers, who were dragging the man toward the church.

Perea looked closely at the captured man's face. He did not recognize him, but that meant nothing.

Perea walked away. Either Renoudot and the others never got on the train, or they got off when the explosion occurred. He could think of no reason why they didn't get on the train. So it must be they got off when the train blew up. Which meant they must still be en route to St. Limoux.

But my God! They cannot come here; the Germans are everywhere, suspicious of everyone.

Perea swore under his breath as he hurried back to the inn.

Renoudot had talked.

He had not wanted to talk, but there is a point where pain becomes more important than the knowledge that one does not want to talk. He had managed not to talk when they tied his testicles with piano wire. He had not talked when they used pliers to pull out his finger nails. After the first three or four he had hardly noticed the pain as they removed the next nail.

The watchful face of the handsome German remained passive. He said a few words now and then and smiled, but Renoudot was beyond the point where words had any meaning. He thought he had passed the point where he could feel more pain.

He was wrong. There is always more pain.

In the end what made him talk were the electrodes.

They attached one to his nose and the other to his penis. And then they sent the electric current coursing through his body. He screamed and thrashed on the table, but the current did not stop. Finally he cried that he would tell them anything, anything at all, if only the pain would stop. His mind no longer was in control. Only his body mattered.

He talked. He babbled. He did not even know what he told the handsome German face that was swimming before him.

"Very good," von Berkow said.

Renoudot stared and tried to focus his eyes. He could not. One eye was crushed from a blow with a lead pipe. The other was hazed over with fluids.

"All this pain," the German was saying. "All this useless pain. I told you I would find out what I wanted to know. You people are so stupid."

At last Renoudot understood what the German was saying. And for the first time he realized what he had done. "I lied," he said, but the words did not come out right because they had knocked out his front teeth with a lead pipe. "I lied," he said again, this time speaking more slowly.

"You didn't lie," the German said. "Men in such agony never lie. They tell the truth."

Renoudot could not remember what he had said. He had tried to be silent. He had tried his best, but sometimes a man's best is not enough.

"I am going to St. Limoux," the German said. "I think I shall be able to find our friends there."

So he had told the truth! The Bergmans were doomed, Renoudot thought, doomed because I talked!

The German smiled. "You have been most helpful. I thank you. And now we must discuss the method of your death."

Renoudot stared at the man's eyes. There was a smile on the face, always this smile, a curling up of the ends of the lips, but the eyes remained cold, cruel, dead.

Von Berkow took out his pistol. "This is the easiest way," he said, cocking the pistol. "It is painless and over in a second."

Renoudot was suddenly angry with himself. He had talked. He was guilty of the most heinous crime in his world. And this stupid German was now expecting him to ask for an easy death. He did not deserve an easy death. And besides, a man has only one death. He should have something to say about it.

"Not the pistol," he said calmly.

"It would be much easier for you."

"You are a swine."

"So be it," the German said, and flicked the switch on the alternator that ran the current to the electrodes. Renoudot screamed and screamed, and in time—there is always death within a certain time—the electric current tortured and exhausted him to a point where his heart gave out, and the jumping body, encrusted in its own sweat and excrement, slumped to the table and did not move anymore. There remained a slight quivering by the nose and penis where the current entered the body from the electrodes, but the man was dead. He had tried desperately to scream something heroic, perhaps "Long Live France," but instead he had again started babbling about the Bergman family and St. Limoux. Such is heroism in the face of unendurable pain.

The German had turned off the switch. He walked quickly from the room with its stench of fear, suffering, and death.

8

The slow clopping of hoofs.

The clanging of pots and pans.

The dogs trotting behind the wagons, making side excursions off the road, dashing back to resume their tireless trotting.

Gypsy laughter.

Two old women shrilly haggling over onions.

Isaac Bergman seated in a wagon. The stoic.

The Basque walked alone on the road, ahead of the first wagon. He did not want to be near the Gypsies and their smell of onions, garlic, and unwashed flesh. He would be glad when they reached St. Limoux tomorrow and he would be rid of these filthy Gypsies. We will go to St. Limoux, and from there we will go straight into the mountains. He looked forward to the clean smell of the mountain air. The perfume of chestnuts and oak.

The pungent odor of pine needles crackling beneath his feet. After a few minutes he realized someone was walking beside him. He turned his head and saw it was the Bergman girl.

They walked in silence for a bit. Finally the girl said, "Does it help to have a stick?"

The Basque looked at her. She was young, with a lean, strong body. But would anyone who asked a question like that about a walking stick survive in the mountains? "Yes. It aids one's balance."

"Will you help me find one?"

"If you wish."

"Thank you, I would appreciate it." She paused, summoned her courage, and continued. "And I want to thank you for what you did last night."

The Basque said nothing.

"It was very kind," she said. "And you are a brave man to be helping us in this way. I'm sorry I acted the way I did. I shouldn't have called you those names."

The Basque shrugged. He was not accustomed to talking with women, but he understood they would say one thing one minute and another the next.

"We are all in your debt," the girl said.

"I am being paid. You owe me nothing."

The girl suddenly spied a long stick by the side of the road. She walked over and picked it up. "Could I use this?" she asked, handing it to him.

The shepherd examined it. "Yes, it will do if I shorten it." He cracked the end over his knee, breaking two feet off the thinner end, tried it out for a few strides, and handed it to the girl. "It will do until we can find a better one."

They walked, and the girl studied the way the man used his stick. She imitated the motions until she had copied them exactly. The two of them walked along for several minutes, the girl's long legs matching the Basque stride for stride. The sticks went forward in unison, hitting the ground with two matching "thumps" and whistling back through the air in common arcs.

"It really makes it easier," she said. "And more fun. Oh, I wish I had learned to do this earlier. It would have made the walks in the *bois* so much more pleasant."

The Basque stared at her with pity. She was a pretty, happy creature who could talk about walks in the *bois* rather than worry about the snow-covered ravines she would have to face in the mountains. He shook his head. The life this girl must have led before this misfortune. A nice big house with warm rooms and hot food. Soft, comfortable beds with huge stuffed pillows. Warm baths. But still she was full of life and courage. He began to hope she would make it through the mountains.

"I did not want to come with my family," she said. "The boy I am to marry, David, was to join us in Toulouse but never arrived."

"Where is he?"

She looked down at the ground as she talked. "God knows. In these times God is the only one who knows anything. I hope David is safe. He is a good person."

"If you like him, he must be a good person," the Basque said softly. It was the first kind word he had spoken to any of the Bergman family. He did not even realize it.

She looked at him and smiled. "Thank you. You have a very kind heart."

The Basque looked straight ahead as he walked. No one had said such a thing to him in years. He was oddly touched.

"Basque is such a strange language," Leah said. "When you and the farmer were talking, I couldn't understand a single word."

The Basque smiled.

"You have a nice smile," she said seriously. "You should do it more often. It helps soften the facial muscles and keeps you from getting wrinkles."

The shepherd almost laughed, something he had not done since, well, something he had not done in years. The girl from the big, comfortable house and the walks in the *bois* was giving him a beauty lesson. "I smiled because you said you did not understand a word of what was said between the farmer and myself."

"Is Basque a difficult language to learn?"

"Very difficult."

"Could you teach me?"

He smiled again, this time the smile coming easier. "There is a legend among our people. The Devil, says the legend, desires to master all the languages of the earth so he may corrupt the souls of all in their native tongue. It is said he spent seven years studying Basque and learned only two words—yes and no."

"That's a fib," she laughed. "But it's a good fib. Basque must have some very hard words to learn. Tell me some of them."

"Only if you say them after me," he said, looking at her with what was almost, but not quite, a twinkle in his eye.

"Of course."

"*Izarysaroyaarenlurrearenbarena.*"

She looked at him with wide eyes. "What does that mean?"

"I thought you were going to repeat it."

"I can't!"

"It means the 'center of the mountain road.'"

"Say something else."

"*Azpilcuetagaraycosaroyarenberecolarrea.*"

"What does *that* mean?"

"The lower ground of the high hill of Azpilcueta."

"What an incredible language! I am glad I was not born a Basque. I would have never learned to talk!"

"If you were born a Basque, you would have had no problem. And you would not call yourself a Basque, either."

"I wouldn't?"

"No. Basque is a word invented by the French or the Spanish. The Spanish also call us the *Vascongados*. Our true name is the one we use among ourselves. It is *Euscaldanac*. It means 'a strong hand.'"

"Is it easy to learn *written* Basque?"

His smile broadened. "There is another legend, a proverb which says when a Basque writes 'Solomon,' he pronounces it 'Nebuchadnezzar.' We are an ancient people. A proud people," he added fiercely.

"But you have managed to survive everything. All the wars, all the conquerors."

He smiled again. "I will give you another bit of wisdom of the *Euscaldanac*. The reason we Basques have survived is we pretend nobody else exists."

They walked along for some minutes, each buried in private thoughts. The Basque taking a quiet joy in his display of knowledge in front of this girl who until now had looked at him with only rage in her eyes. He had seen the fires of rage die, and he was content. He did not know why. The girl meant nothing to him. She was only someone he was leading into the mountains to die. He was certain she would die. They would all die. It would not be his fault. It was the fault of the fools who expected people like this to go through the mountains in the snow. Fools! Stupid people who did not understand the mountains or the cold. Soft men who lived in towns and said, "Let us do this," and because they had said it, they expected it could be done. But what men wanted to do and what human flesh could do were often not the same.

"I hope David is safe," the girl said in a voice that quivered.

The Basque nodded his head. Although he had felt no compassion for many years, once he had known this emotion as well as any man, and so he understood. "I am sure he is safe. *Fain Goicoa* will look after him."

"What were those words you said?"

"*Fain Goicoa*. In the language of the *Euscaldanac* it means 'The Good Master On High.' It is the way we refer to God."

"Leah!" a voice called from the second wagon. The girl turned and saw her mother peering out. "Leah, come here, please. I need your help."

"I must go," the girl said. "Thank you for the stick. And for everything else. But I won't be satisfied until you teach me to speak Basque." She waited for the second wagon to come alongside and disappeared in the darkened interior.

The Basque shook his head. If the mother needed help even while riding in the wagon, she would never get far in the mountains.

It was too bad about the girl. There would be no problem if she were the only one. But she is not the only one; there is the rest of her family, and she will never leave them.

A dog raced past, barking loudly, chasing a field rodent, followed by three small boys. One of the women shouted for them to stop, and the fat Gypsy woke up with a start, yelling at the woman for disturbing his rest. His shouting woke a baby, who began to cry.

The Basque shook his head. He walked more quickly to get farther in front of this pack of *animals*.

It was getting darker as they came closer to the mountains, and even at this distance the cold coming down from the peaks chilled the bones. The fingers of death reaching out.

It was getting darker. And colder.

"Stop! We camp here for the night," the fat Gypsy cried out as they came to a grove of trees near the side of the road.

The wagons clattered to a stop. The women immediately began to prepare the evening meal.

The Basque walked a little way off and sat down, his back resting against a tree.

Samuel Bergman sat apart from the others, waiting for his supper and, like the Basque, worried about the days ahead in the mountain crossing. He was fifteen years old, and he had always limped from the time he caught polio as a little child. One leg had not grown as long as the other. And while he had learned to get along with a shortened leg, he had never developed an interest in anything physical. Instead, he had become like his father, bookish, introspective, haunting libraries and shops of booksellers whenever he had free time. His father encouraged him in the pursuit of matters of the mind.

He had adored his father. No matter how much he studied about a subject, his father always had known more. There was no end to his father's storehouse of knowledge. *How lucky I am.* To grow up in a house with a mind like this. There is so much I wish to know. There is so much knowledge to learn that I do not even know what I do not know.

His father, at times, allowed him to sit in the study while he was entertaining friends, and Samuel was never so happy as when he was listening to some famous professor of philosophy from Belgium or Italy or a doctor of letters from some other capital of the world.

Now, with all that had happened, he wondered if any of his old values had any meaning. His mother interrupted his thoughts when she brought him a bowl of soup.

Listlessly he swallowed a few spoonfuls. It didn't taste very good, but it was warm, and he finished it.

After his mother had taken the empty bowl, Samuel walked through the tiny camp. He noticed the Basque off by himself. A strange man. Yet, Samuel thought, a man who seems perfectly capable of taking care of himself, while my father and the rest of my family seem quite incapable. He remembered his sister coming back to the wagon earlier and saying the shepherd seemed very nice. "That one?" his mother had said with scorn. "Don't tell me he isn't an animal."

Samuel puzzled on this. He walked closer, wanting to talk with him.

"If you are through with the bowl, sir, I will take it back to the women," he said to the Basque.

The Basque nodded. "Take it."

"It wasn't very good soup."

"There is life in soup that is good, but when one is hungry, there is life in soup that is not very good, too."

Instead of picking up the bowl, the boy sat down. "You don't like my family, do you?"

The Basque took the pipe out of his mouth. He did not say anything.

"I'm sorry you don't like us. My sister says she likes you."

Another silence.

Samuel persisted. "I don't blame you for not liking us. I know, from my geography lessons, what the mountains are like. I know you think it is an impossible task to get us across. We are weaklings, all of us."

The Basque's voice was soft. "We are what life has made us. Do not blame yourself."

"I have always been taught that the only thing that is important is the mind. Now I know this is wrong. Now it is important for us to cross the mountains, and we have not prepared ourselves to do it."

The Basque nodded. He was strangely troubled by the young boy's words. It was what he had been saying to himself all along, but saying it to himself was one thing, and hearing it from a young boy who spoke the words with bitterness was another.

"It is strange," Samuel continued, almost as if he were thinking aloud, "until now I never had any regard for physical strength, but now it is the only thing that matters. You are strong. You will cross the mountains. My father is weak. He will die, and then what good will all his books do him?"

"A boy should not talk against his father."

"Why not? All my life he told me things would be one way, and now none of it is true. And now I will die. We will all die because my father lied to himself and lied to me!"

"Stop!" the Basque said angrily. "I will not listen to a son talk like this about his father. Your father did what he thought best for you. If it is not, do not blame him. No man is perfect."

The boy cowered before the shepherd's harsh voice, but he knew in his heart that he was speaking the truth. His father had told him it was a world of the mind. What did the mind matter to a German with a machine gun? His father had been his hero because he was intelligent and witty. He had been wrong. His hero should have been someone like this Basque, who carried a heavy stick, and who, with a word, could make that Gypsy who had been bothering his sister slink away like a dog with his tail between his legs.

"A man has only one father in this life," the Basque said. "Remember that."

"I'm sorry. I did not mean to attack him. It's just that for the first time in my life I realize that books are not everything."

"Books are not everything. Nothing is everything."

Samuel hesitated. He said at last: "If we get through the mountains, will you teach me to be a shepherd like yourself?"

"It is a hard life. You know nothing about it."

"I'm only fifteen years old. I am young enough to learn to do anything for the rest of my life."

The Basque puffed his pipe. The problem was not that the boy wasn't young enough to learn; the problem was the mountains. He will never grow old enough to learn anything because he will not live much longer. It is too bad. The boy, like his sister, had courage and a strong heart. But a strong heart does not carry one across the mountains. For that, one needs strong legs.

"What is wrong with your leg?"

"A disease when I was three years old. The doctors could do nothing. It never grew as long as the other."

"Can you climb?"

"Yes. I climbed trees in the *bois*. Even with this leg."

"Does it tire you?"

"Not badly. I cannot run, but I can climb, and I can keep moving for a long time."

"Do you think you can climb through the mountains?"

The boy was quiet.

"They are steep. There are many loose rocks. It is cold, and there will be snow. Do you think you can do it?"

"I can try."

The Basque was thoughtful. "If you try hard enough and want to do it enough, you may do it."

"Thank you," Samuel said. "I will try because it is the only way I will survive." He limped back toward his family.

The shepherd watched him go. First the sister, now this one. What was the matter with him? Angrily he wrapped himself in his heavy coat, rolled over on his side, and went to sleep.

Samuel curled up in the corner of the wagon next to his sister, who was already asleep.

He had told the Basque he wanted to be a shepherd. Why had he said that? Samuel, the son of Isaac Bergman, a shepherd? Everyone would laugh. Then he caught himself. No one would laugh because everyone he knew would probably be dead. The old life was over, done with. Never again would he listen to lies. He would become strong like the Basque, and no Gypsy would humiliate him the way that pig humiliated his father.

He admitted to himself that he held his father in contempt. Tears came to his eyes. He had always loved his father, respected him as the authority on everything. And now he knew he had been wrong. He was not so much angry with his father as angry with himself for being so naïve. He began to cry softly.

His sister woke up. "What's the matter?"

Silence.

"Why are you crying?"

Silence.

"Please tell me. I want to help."

Samuel did not answer. Quietly he sobbed himself to sleep.

9

The next day the caravan was on the road. The fat Gypsy was in fine spirits. He whistled and hummed as the horse plodded along. The Basque sat beside him.

"Have you seen my daughter Carla? The one with the full belly," the fat Gypsy asked.

The Basque nodded.

"Soon she will give me another grandson." After a pause he asked, "Do you have a family?"

"No."

"That is too bad. A family is a good thing."

The Basque was silent.

"You are missing a great deal in life, my friend, a great deal. When the whole world is falling apart, and you have a family, there is always someplace to go, someone you can trust and who will take care of you."

The Basque stared at the fat Gypsy until the man

became uncomfortable. He looked away and became interested in the reins leading to the horse. They passed along the fields on the dirt road. The branches of the trees and shrubs were preparing for winter. Their leaves had dropped, and the gnarled wood stood exposed.

Later in the day a group of peasants came down the road.

"You are going to St. Limoux?" one of the men asked as they drew abreast.

"Yes," the fat Gypsy said.

"Watch out for the Germans."

"Germans?"

"There was a train wreck. Sabotage."

"The Germans are blaming everyone. Watch out."

"Many thanks."

The Basque listened carefully to this conversation. He looked at the fat Gypsy, who leaned inside the wagon and spoke a few words to someone. Then he turned back to the Basque and said, "I think this is as far as we are going. There are Germans in St. Limoux. You heard the talk about the train wreck? Who knows, the Germans may decide to blame it on us."

"I must get to St. Limoux."

The fat Gypsy threw up his hands. "Who is stopping you?"

The wagons pulled off the road, and the Gypsies busied themselves about their new campsite. The Bergman family stood off by themselves.

Another cart of peasants came from the direction of St. Limoux. "Gypsies! If you are going to St. Limoux, be careful. The Germans are arresting people."

"Because of the train?"

"Yes, the train."

"What are they doing with the people they arrest?"

"Who knows? They put them in the church."

"The church!" the fat Gypsy said, and then he swore under his breath. He went to the back of the second wagon and demanded something to eat.

What do we do now, the Basque thought. Perea would be waiting with supplies and mountain-climbing gear in St. Limoux. Without warm clothes and boots these Jews wouldn't last five hours in the mountains.

"What is happening?" Professor Bergman asked.

"This is as far as they go."

"Maybe we can go into the mountains from here."

The Basque shook his head. "There is no pass here. We must go to St. Limoux."

The Basque thought. Yes, they could do that. But the Germans would wonder about the sight of five strangely dressed people walking into town from nowhere. And if anyone took the trouble to look closely, they would notice the man and his son looked like Jews. If the Gypsies were with them, the Bergmans might go unnoticed.

The Basque made his decision. He walked over to the fat Gypsy. "We want you to take us to St. Limoux."

The fat Gypsy looked annoyed. "You heard about the Germans. We stay here."

"We will pay."

A crafty look crossed the fat Gypsy's face. "Do they have money?" he asked, jerking his thumb in the direction of the Bergman family.

"I have money."

"I thought you said they had not paid you?"

The Basque tapped his *makhila* against the fat Gypsy's chest. "I said I have the money."

"How much will you pay us if we do this for you?"

"Five hundred pesetas."

"Huh, that is not enough to ask a man to risk his life," the Gypsy said, beginning the bargaining. "Two thousand."

The Basque had been watching the man closely. He was satisfied with the reaction. If he asked for two thousand he would settle for one thousand. This was the figure he had in mind from the beginning. He remembered that Renoudot had promised him another four thousand. Perea might object, but there was nothing he could do. It was another four thousand, or he would abandon them all. Of this four thousand he would spend one thousand to get the Gypsies to take them to St. Limoux.

"It is not a risk of your life."

The Gypsy shrugged. "Fifteen hundred."

"We also need clothes."

"Clothes?" the Fat Gypsy said, perplexed. "What clothes are you talking about?"

"Gypsy clothes. If we go into St. Limoux together, we should all look as if we are one group."

"They cost money."

"We will pay."

"Clothes are very expensive."

The Basque tapped him with his *makhila*. "I do not wish to argue. "Seven hundred and fifty pesetas."

"Fourteen hundred."

"Eight hundred, fifty."

"Twelve hundred. And you are asking me to risk my life."

"One thousand pesetas. My final offer."

"A hard bargain. Make it another fifty. One thousand and fifty."

"Very well. One thousand and fifty."

The Basque reached into his pocket, turning sideways to conceal the bills from the Gypsy. "I will give it to you now."

He turned back and handed the money to the Gypsy. "Here. Now bring the clothes."

The fat Gypsy took the money and waddled over to the caravan. "Hurry!" he shouted. "We go to St. Limoux." He climbed up on the first wagon and disappeared inside.

The Basque walked over to Bergman. "We are going to St. Limoux. All of us."

"What made him change his mind?" Bergman asked.

The Basque shrugged. "Who knows?"

"I saw him pay that Gypsy," Samuel whispered to his sister.

"I know. I saw it, too."

The fat Gypsy came back with an armload of clothing. "Here," he said, holding out a dress and a vest to the girl. "It belongs to my daughter when she doesn't have her belly. It should fit you. Here is a hat, too." And he went about distributing the clothes.

When they came out from behind the trees, the Fat Gypsy roared with laughter. "What fine Gypsies you make! Ah-ha, and you," he said, pinching the girl on the elbow, "what a beautiful Gypsy girl you have turned out to be! Better not let my son see you, ha!"

The Basque put on his vest and scarf and cap. Another Gypsy. He could pass anywhere. The Bergman family converged on him. "Do we really look like Gypsies?" the boy asked.

"If no one looks too closely," the father said.

The Basque eyed them critically. The girl was perfect, right down to the dark eyes and the flashing teeth.

"I feel indecent," she said, tugging at the low-cut neck.

"Better than being dead," the Basque said.

He looked at the boy, who was dressed in a nondescript outfit that was half rags. Good. The mother looked like all the other older fat Gypsy women in their baggy, colorful outfits. The only problem was the father. The clothes were good, but no Gypsy looked the way he did.

"You don't look like a Gypsy," the Basque said.

"I have had very little training."

"Go in the wagon and get under the blankets. Pretend to be sick. If anyone comes over to you, act like you are dying. And take off your spectacles."

Isaac Bergman obeyed. He went into the second wagon and crawled under a filthy blanket. A Gypsy girl who was nursing a baby stared at him. Bergman was embarrassed and turned his face to the side of the wagon. The girl continued to nurse her baby.

"We are ready," the fat Gypsy announced as the wagons continued their journey to St. Limoux.

It was late in the afternoon when the German staff car sped along the road from Toulouse to St. Limoux. It raised a cloud of dust that blew across the fields. The peasants who were working in the fields looked up with expressions of distaste when they saw the swastika pennant on the fender.

Captain von Berkow slouched in the back seat, his hat pulled down lower than usual. He was annoyed with himself. Bergman should have been captured in Toulouse, and now, because the man had escaped, he had to go to some godforsaken town named St. Limoux.

He felt superior to this sort of work.

The von Berkows were landed people, a family of *Junkers*, aristocrats who, along with others of their class, held Prussia as a personal fief. They had their castle and their lands. The von Berkows had been a military family for four hundred years, pillars of Prussian militarism and the General Staff, disciples of Scharnhorst and Gneisenau and von Moltke. As far as the family was concerned, Gunther was not properly following the tradition because he was not in the regular army but in the

SS. A Von Berkow belonged in the army, the real army, not the political army of this Bohemian corporal. The man was an upstart. However, things were as they were, and one made the best of them.

Young Gunther looked like the other von Berkows whose portraits lined the stone corridors of the drafty ancestral home. Big, handsome men who glowered from behind heavy moustaches, mutton chops, and complicated sword trappings. Helmut Christian von Berkow, who ruled the manor in the eighteenth century, had had his portrait painted showing him on a rearing horse. He had his sword unsheathed and was holding it aloft. It was the family joke. Helmut Christian suffered from a disease that paralyzed his legs when he was ten, and he never rode a horse after that, much less led a cavalry charge. He was driven to prove his manhood by taking two women at a time and beating peasants to death with a horsewhip. He would have the hapless victim tied to the heavy rings above the fireplace and whip him in front of the dancing flames.

Helmut Christian was the family joke, but they never told any outsider about him. Nothing could even be whispered that detracted from the family's long history of faithful and honorable service to Prussia.

Perhaps the peculiarities in Gunther could be traced to his ancestor, Helmut Christian. As a boy, Gunther delighted in killing cats and driving red-hot nails into frogs. He would lock up a dog in some hidden room in the manor and leave him to starve. He would trap birds, break their wings, and put them in a room with a cat. The cat always took its time in getting to the inevitable. That was the part that fascinated the boy. How long it took and how many ways there were to prolong the final act, the ultimate moment, the instant of death.

Born in 1911, a red thing covered with birth fluids, he

was born an Officer into a family of Officers who served Kaiser Wilhelm in his dream to continue the work started by the War of 1870. He was seven years old in 1918 when Germany fell to her knees and Kaiser Wilhelm was exposed as a fraud who had led his people to disaster.

Hard times came to the *Junkers* of Prussia, the way they came to the rest of Germany. The von Berkows stayed in their hinterland retreat but could not escape the great waves of inflation, unemployment, poverty, and the afflictions of a conquered nation that swept across the country. In 1928 Gunther was sent to school in Munich because his father said the family needed a man who understood the finances of the world. Of course, he would eventually go into the army.

In Munich Gunther could not help becoming involved in the violent political arguments that were held on the street corners, in the beer halls, in cafés, in homes, everywhere. Munich was a seething political discussion from sunup to sundown and beyond. Intellectuals sat huddled around small stoves, arguing and talking through the nights.

But talk was only talk, and what was needed was far more than talk.

One day, early in 1929, young Gunther was taken to a small apartment at 41 Thierschstrasse to meet a rising political figure named Adolf Hitler. The aristocratic von Berkow was not very impressed by the man. He looked and sounded like a fanatic. He had no ancestral castle with pictures of forebears on the walls, no generals of the same name, and even worse, he had served in the war as an enlisted man. A corporal! If this political figure had shown up at home in Prussia, his father would have sent him to eat and sleep with the servants. It was even rumored the man was a bastard.

After the election of March 1930, Gunther realized he

had underestimated this politician. His party won a considerable number of seats in the Reichstag, and many important businessmen were beginning to give him their backing. In a Germany that was stunned and beaten to its knees, he alone seemed to have a definite program. He alone seemed to be sure of his answers.

The terrible effects of the worldwide depression helped Hitler. There was poverty in every country. Breadlines, soup kitchens, men with no work to do and no hope of getting work. Women who were helpless as they watched their men slowly withdraw into shells, rarely even trying to get work anymore, talking less, doing less. The children tried to eat the paint off the walls and died from the lead in it. If a coat was ripped, it had to be sewed. If the soles of shoes wore through, they had to be repaired with cardboard. If a dish broke, well, one made do with one less dish. If a child died, it was buried in a pauper's grave. A faint prayer went to heaven: Maybe she is at peace now; maybe there is enough to eat up there.

Everyone was asking questions, but few men had answers.

The corporal had answers, and he told them to anyone who would listen. Anyone who listened once would listen again. The rallies became larger and larger, the orator better and better. A great movement was taking shape, and Gunther was right in the middle of it.

His friends arranged another meeting with the leader of National Socialism. Another man, Heinrich Himmler, was present, and he became very excited over the pure Nordic looks of the young Prussian nobleman. This, he said, is an example of running true to blood type. Himmler took over the young man's career, and in such a way did Gunther find himself wearing a black uniform, a member of the select SS.

Once in a while he thought about the leader and the party he served, but he never worried too much about it. To him it was not a question of politics but of the survival of the fatherland, the protection of the topsoil of Bavaria, the prosperity of the industrial guts of the Ruhr, the sanctity of the memory of his ancestors on the walls of his castle. Germany was in trouble, and the leader and his party worked to save it. There were injustices, but these were as nothing compared to the injustice being done to the fatherland. He felt his judgment was vindicated when Adolf Hitler became chancellor of the Reich.

His fortunes rose rapidly because he had a very important friend in the newly created SS Reichsführer, Heinrich Himmler. He had personal access to this man whose name was becoming known and feared throughout Germany. If Hitler was the word, Himmler was becoming known as the deed. His black-shirted troopers swaggered down the streets and unified Germany behind the leader. Their methods were simple. You supported Hitler, or they carried you off to their personal torture chambers and made you see the error of your ways. In time they needed more room than a building in the middle of the city could afford, so they set up camps in places like Sachsenhausen, Ravensbruck, Buchenwald, and Dachau. In the solitude of these places they could torture prisoners until they fell down from the exhaustion of inflicting so much pain.

When Himmler created the super-select SD in 1931, he found a key post for the young Prussian nobleman. He discovered the man had a talent for convincing people to talk. This function was very important in the new Reich because there were still a great many enemies within the country, and it was vital to get them out of the way.

Gunther did his work quietly and thoroughly and became a captain. Even though he was only a captain, his personal influence with Himmler exceeded that of most generals. When Austria, Czechoslovakia, and Poland ceased to exist, he was sent to detain and question certain important people. When Paris fell, he found himself on the same errand.

It had been more difficult to round up suspects in France. This Bergman thing had made him look foolish. The man was a fuzzy-thinking intellectual, a writer, a Jew, the easiest sort to arrest because they were so busy theorizing about the world they forgot about the realities of club and gun. Bergman had gotten away, but it was obvious that others had planned it. The Underground again.

He thought about what the Bergman family might be planning to do *after* St. Limoux. Could they be on their way to the sea? He took out a map and studied it. The sea seemed unlikely. Why would they go from Toulouse to St. Limoux if they were planning to go to the sea? St. Limoux lay in the wrong direction. So where do they go from St. Limoux? He studied the map briefly and came to the obvious conclusion. *The mountains.* St. Limoux lay snuggled at the base of the mountains.

The mountains? At this time of year?

Could it be possible they were considering crossing the mountains? They would risk death in a dozen ways, he thought. But it is also the one place where pursuit will be the most difficult and the chances of finding them the slightest. Once they get deep into the mountains, we may never find them.

He was in a foul mood as the car swerved around a corner and came toward a caravan of horse-drawn wagons.

Von Berkow pulled himself forward in the seat to get a better look. He saw a group of Gypsy wagons driving down the road, moving slowly, leisurely.

He watched through the window as the car passed. One didn't get to see Gypsies in Germany anymore. They had all either fled the country or were in concentration camps.

The car passed around a bend, and the Gypsies were lost to his view.

St. Limoux was only a few minutes away.

10

The town was a madhouse.

The Germans were arresting everyone in sight.

A man with a flock of chickens was arrested.

One old woman began hitting a policeman when he tried to take her husband, and he arrested her, too.

A farmer, driving a pair of oxen, was arrested. The oxen wandered off.

The prisoners were taken to the church and herded through the twenty-foot-high iron-bound doors. Bullet marks pocked the whitewashed walls around the doors, mementos of other times of trial.

At the inn, the proprietor was in a frenzy. He did not have enough help to serve the curious farmers who were staying in town to watch the show or the heavy influx of German soldiers.

Perea was seated at a table near the window when the

proprietor came up to him. "M'sieu, have you been served?"

"No."

The proprietor wrung his hands together. "All these people . . . I just don't have enough help."

A sudden thought occurred to Perea. With all the Germans in town, suspicious about the sabotage, it would not be a bad idea for him to have a safe cover.

"Do you need another waiter?" he asked.

The proprietor did not understand. "What? A waiter? Of course I could use another waiter." His voice became annoyed, and he said, "Now if you would be good enough to tell me what you want."

"I will be your waiter."

For a moment the idea seemed to puzzle the proprietor. Finally he understood and smiled. "Good, good," he said. "Come with me and I will get you an apron. You serve only the drinks. The girls will take care of the food."

Perea took off his coat and put on the dirty white apron.

"You go to each table and ask what they want. Come back and tell me. I give you the orders, and you take them out. Simple, yes?"

"Ha!" said one of the serving girls as she passed by with a tray of food. "The Germans will drive you crazy. All they want is beer, beer, beer, the filthy swine."

"Annette!" the proprietor said. And then in a whisper, "Will you shut up. They might hear."

"What do I care?"

Perea coughed, and the proprietor looked nervously at him. "Pay no mind, m'sieu. Annette has her little joke, but she means no harm. We are all loyal people here."

"As loyal as myself, no doubt," Perea said, going into the main room.

He took orders and delivered them. It was easy work, and as he had told himself, not one German bothered to look at him except to ask for something to drink. Once two French policemen came in and questioned a few customers, but no one paid him the slightest attention. It was as if he were a chair or a table. He was a fixture. Fixtures are not suspected of anything.

At this time an SS officer entered the room, walked over to an empty table near the window, and sat down. Perea tugged at his apron and went over.

"May I bring you something to drink, sir?"

The officer regarded him for a few seconds. Then he smiled. "Why, yes, something to drink would be nice. Do you have any beer?"

Perea nodded.

"Bring me a beer."

Perea went into the back and found the proprietor. "Do you see what we have outside? An SS officer, a captain, I think."

"The SS!" the proprietor said "My God, what is he doing here?"

"He's thirsty. He wants a beer."

"Here," he said, shoving a bottle and glass at Perea. "Tell him with the compliments of the house."

Perea poured the beer and smiled at the SS officer. "The proprietor wishes you to enjoy this with the compliments of the house, sir."

"That's very nice. Thank him for me."

"Yes, sir," Perea said, turning away.

"One moment, please," the German said. "You do have a moment, don't you?" he asked very politely.

"Uh, yes, of course, sir," Perea said.

"The train wreck seems to be causing a bit of commotion, doesn't it?"

"Yes, sir. This is usually a very sleepy town."

"Ahhh," the German said, looking out the window. "But now it does not seem to sleep at all." He turned back to Perea. "Have you seen many people around who are not usually here?"

Perea felt an inward release of tension. The SS man was assuming that he had always worked here at the inn.

"No, sir. Only farmers. Men with goods to trade. Nothing strange. Until, of course . . ."

The German smiled. "Until, of course, the train wreck, and since then there have been a great many strange faces. Yes, yes, I understand."

The German stared out the window for a few moments. "Did you see the people who got off the train, the one that was wrecked?"

"The people, sir?"

"Yes. Surely you went to the station. How did the passengers arrive?"

"Hand cars, sir. When the news of the sabotage reached the authorities, they sent hand cars to bring the passengers here."

"Describe them."

"Describe what, sir? The hand cars?"

The German smiled. "No, not the hand cars. The passengers. What did they look like?"

Perea began to sweat. "They were just people, sir. Many of them were injured. There was a gendarme with a broken arm. A young girl who cried all the time. Just people, sir. Even a few dead bodies."

"I see," the German said, looking out the window again. Perea waited for a full minute, but the German ignored him. Finally he walked away, busying himself with empty glasses. After a few minutes he walked back to the officer.

"Another beer, sir?"

"No, thank you."

"Something to eat?"

"A bit later."

"Very good, sir." A pause. "I have noticed you keep looking out the window. Has anything new happened?"

The German devoted all his attention to Perea. "No, nothing out of the ordinary."

"I thought perhaps they might have caught some of the saboteurs by now."

"Are you interested in saboteurs?"

Perea shrugged. "This is quite a big event around here. Who could not be interested?"

The German thought for a moment, then said, "Of course. No, as far as I know, they have not caught any saboteurs. But then I don't really know everything that's going on."

"Aren't you in charge of the investigation, sir?"

"No. I am not involved. Trains, it seems, come under the military jurisdiction."

The German looked up and noticed that Perea was staring at him. "So now you are wondering what I am doing here, eh?" He laughed softly. "Waiters and hotel desk clerks are the nosiest people in the world. No, my friend, I am not here about the train. It is another matter."

Perea smiled nervously and then looked out the window. A Gypsy caravan was coming down the street. Perea watched them with little interest until something about one of the gypsies on the buckboard of the first wagon stopped him. Where had he seen that face before?

Mother of God!! It was the Basque!

The Gypsy caravan clattered down the street, the pots and pans making a racket. The heads of children peered out from openings in the wagons, gazing out at the wonders of the town.

"Gypsies," the German captain said, looking at the

caravan. "Almost as much of a nuisance as the Jews. Inferior blood. Tell me," he said, turning to Perea, the smile missing for the first time, "do many Gypsies pass through this town?"

"No more than any other town in this part of the country, sir."

The German got up. "I think I will take a look for myself." He turned to a table where four Wehrmacht soldiers sat, trying to avoid his gaze. "You can stop pretending that I am not here," the captain said. "Please go out and stop those Gypsies."

The four men jumped to their feet, grabbed their rifles, and ran out the door. They didn't bother to pay their bill. Perea did not feel it was the time to detain them.

"Well," said the German officer, his smile back again, "thank you for the beer. And the conversation. I'll be back later for more of both."

Perea watched him go out the door.

Now what do I do? Run? Stay here?

Mother of God!

Gunther von Berkow walked slowly toward the Gypsy wagons, regarding them with a critical eye. One of the mangy dogs came a few steps forward, sniffed, whined, and slunk back under a cart. The four soldiers stood in front of the first wagon, their rifles cradled in their arms. The captain looked at the two men on the seat. One was grossly fat. Pig, he thought. Only a pig could let his body get like that.

"Where are you going?"

"To the west, sir," the fat Gypsy said hoarsely.

"How many of you are there?"

The fat Gypsy thought for a moment and then said,

"Maybe twenty-five, thirty or so, including the children."

"Don't you know the exact number?"

"People come and go, sir. It is never the same number."

Pigs, he thought for the second time. Roving animals who travel around in packs. Scum! We will get around to them soon enough.

"What's your business here?"

"Only passing through, sir. We thought we might sing and dance for the people, put on a little show. They will give us money and food, sir. This is how we earn our living."

"I want none of that here."

"If you say so, sir, no singing and dancing," said the fat Gypsy in a cringing whine. He was sweating heavily, although the air was cool and crisp.

The captain came closer and stared at the Basque. This is a different sort, the Captain thought. "Don't tell me you sing and dance?"

The Basque looked directly into the German's eyes. "No. I do none of those things." He jerked his thumb at the fat Gypsy. "I am his brother."

Your brother should try to keep his body the way you keep yours, von Berkow thought. He climbed up on the step and peered into the wagon. A frightened woman shrank back as a small boy started to whimper. The captain's eyes came to Meriam Bergman. The eyes moved on. Samuel sat next to her in his rags and torn cap. The German didn't give him a second glance. Another filthy Gypsy urchin who was learning to steal and cheat like his elders. With any luck for us, the captain thought, he'll never live to be a man.

He passed to the second wagon. A woman sat nursing a baby beside a little girl who was holding a rag doll.

"Is that your doll?" the captain asked.

The girl pulled the doll close to her chest, making herself as small as possible.

"I won't take it away. It is a very nice doll."

"I have a carved wooden dog," a little boy said, jealous of the attention being paid his sister.

"May I see it?"

The boy reached into the torn pocket of his jacket and pulled out the wooden dog and bravely offered it to the German, who took it and examined it closely. The boy's mother, on the other side of the wagon, looked on with horror, terrified that her son was bringing attention to them.

The German handed the dog back to the boy. "He is a very nice dog. Take good care of him."

Walking along the outside, he passed to the farther end of the wagon and stopped when he saw a man who was covered with blankets. A very pretty Gypsy girl stood near the back of the wagon next to the man.

"What's wrong with this one?" he asked the girl.

"He is very sick," she said quietly.

"Sick? With what?"

"Who knows? He has been sick for weeks."

"He is your father?"

"Yes," Leah Bergman answered truthfully.

He regarded the girl. She was very pretty. "What is your name?" he asked.

"Marie," she lied.

He smiled at her. She did not smile back.

He turned his attention to the man under the blankets. The man looked up and moaned softly. He had a heavy woolen cap pulled over his forehead. His shirt and vest were filthy.

"So, Gypsy, are you cold?" von Berkow said, pulling down the blanket.

The man tried to pull the blanket back, but von Berkow grabbed his hand. The German regarded the puny hand with distaste.

Leah was horrified when she saw her father's hand in the grasp of the SS captain. She had to distract him. She moved closer to the man, brushing her shoulder against his arm.

The captain turned, a blank look on his face until he saw the coquettish pose of the girl. He dropped Bergman's hand. It quickly disappeared under the blanket.

Von Berkow turned and faced the girl. She stood firm while his hand reached out and stroked the smooth skin of her cheek. He reached out, insolently, and untied the bow at the top of her plunging neckline. He pulled the strings apart and looked at the further expanse of flesh. Leah did not move. The smile remained on her face.

Meriam Bergman let out a gasp and started to move forward when she felt a strong hand grasp her shoulder. She looked up into the eyes of the Basque. He shook his head. Meriam's hand came to her mouth, but she did not try to go to her daughter.

Von Berkow looked straight into the girl's eyes for a few seconds and then, without warning, struck out with the palm of his hand and caught the girl full in the face, knocking her off her feet and onto the ground.

Meriam again tried to move forward, but the Basque pushed her back, and he went to the girl's side. He reached down and helped her get slowly to her feet. There was a red welt on her face and fear in her eyes.

Von Berkow watched the Basque help the girl to her feet. He looked at the Basque, and their eyes met and held for a brief time. Finally the captain lost interest, turned, and went back to the fat Gypsy.

"Are you the leader?" he asked.

"I . . . well . . . I suppose . . . yes, most of the time."

"Are you or aren't you?"

"Yes, sir," the fat Gypsy said miserably. These Germans, he was thinking, have a way of picking out the leaders and shooting them.

"Good. I hold you responsible for the entire group," Von Berkow said. He was troubled by them. There was something about that sick old man that bothered him. Something about those Gypsies that seemed wrong. "Don't leave town until I tell you," he added.

"Yes, but please, sir, for how long? It is only by traveling from place to place that we are able to make our living, poor and stingy as it may be."

"Not long. I will tell you."

"Yes, sir," the fat Gypsy said unhappily.

The captain turned and walked toward the church. *What swine Gypsies are!*

He came to the entrance of the church, and the two Wehrmacht guards saluted. He returned the salute and stepped through the slightly opened door. In the murky light he could see forty or fifty men sitting and lying on the floor.

At the front of the church a Wehrmacht lieutenant and a French police officer sat at a table questioning a prisoner. Von Berkow stopped at the altar rail and listened.

"But if you can't prove where you were, how can we know that you are not one of the saboteurs?" the lieutenant said.

"I can prove it. I was in my home. If you will only get my wife and ask her. She will tell you."

"She will lie for you," said the policeman.

"But how else can I prove I was home? There was only my wife and the three children. Ask the children. They will tell you."

"We do not accept the testimony of children."

The suspect wrung his hands together. "Then how can I prove I am innocent?"

"You should have thought of that before you blew up the train?"

"I have never done such a thing! I have never broken the law in my life."

The French policeman leaned forward. "A man who protests he has never broken the law is surely guilty of breaking it many times."

"When did you join the Underground?" the lieutenant asked.

The Frenchman rocked back in his chair. "Join the . . . but, sir! I am not a member of the Underground. I spit on that group!" he said, and true to his word, spat on the floor.

"Enough of that!" the French officer said.

"But I am innocent!"

"Guilty!"

"No, no, I protest! I am a farmer, only a farmer!"

"Who else is in the Underground with you?"

"I am innocent."

Amateurs, Von Berkow thought. How do they expect to find out anything if they act this way? These French will tell lies forever. To get them to admit the truth, you have to strip away their self-assurance, reduce them to shells of their former selves. Do this and they will tell you anything, even that their own mothers are members of the Underground.

"Take this one away," the lieutenant said. He glanced up and noticed von Berkow.

"Heil Hitler."

"Heil Hitler," the captain said in a bored voice. "I am Captain von Berkow. How are your investigations coming along?"

The lieutenant stood up and bowed slightly as he introduced himself. "I am Lieutenant Reincke, and this gentleman from the French authorities is Lieutenant Garai."

The Frenchman bowed and said, "So far we have uncovered nothing."

"It takes time," the Wehrmacht lieutenant added.

Von Berkow nodded that he understood. "Yes, I know. Do you have any serious suspects?"

"Not yet," the lieutenant said.

"How about that one you were just questioning?"

The lieutenant shrugged. "He's innocent. Only a farmer who came to town because he was curious."

"Did he tell you that?"

"Yes."

"And you believed him?"

"Not because he said it. He's just such a bumbling fool. How could a man like that plan to sabotage a train."

Fine, von Berkow thought. Now all anyone has to do to prove their innocence is to act the part of the fool.

"Have you thought about using more drastic methods?"

The lieutenant looked puzzled.

"Something more physical," Von Berkow explained.

"Is that necessary?"

"It speeds up the process."

"The Wehrmacht is not accustomed to such methods, Captain," the lieutenant said stiffly.

God save us from the Wehrmacht and their stupid codes of honor, von Berkow thought.

"Even when it is a question of sabotage, and the safety of the fatherland is at stake?"

The lieutenant understood. "We will think about it."

Von Berkow smiled. "Good luck, Lieutenant." He returned the salutes of the two officers and left the church.

He smiled again. They will be lucky if they find anyone who admits to being anywhere within fifty kilometers of the train. He decided it was time for dinner and walked toward the inn.

II

It was dark.

Isaac Bergman remained on the floor of the wagon, covered by the dirty blanket, shivering, possessed with a senseless fear that penetrated his bones. He could not get the German's face out of his mind.

It was a handsome face. A smooth-shaven face, aristocratic, Teutonic. But Isaac Bergman had looked deep into it and knew it was a face of death. There was no doubt in his mind. He had seen an evil he had never seen before. He shuddered. He felt his hand. The German had held it, and it would never be the same again. He would feel that grip for the rest of his life.

He began to believe he would never escape and despised himself for his cowardice. He knew his son was aware of his fear and was beginning to spend more and more time away from him and with the Basque shepherd.

Isaac Bergman was a philosopher. But being a philosopher and a philosophical man are two different matters. The first is a theoretician, the second a realist. Rarely are the theoreticians realistic, he thought. Rather, the opposite. The theoreticians were always constructing worlds that did not work, while the philosophical men, the realists, were creating ways to work within the worlds that existed.

He could not accept that he was losing his son to this Basque shepherd. He could not believe that his son looked at him with scorn.

He turned his face toward the side of the wagon and wept.

"Father, what is it?" asked the daughter, Leah.

"Nothing, nothing," he said.

"But you're crying."

"I am not," he said, stifling the tears.

"You are."

"I was thinking about all the poor Jews who are dead," he said.

"Crying won't help them."

"But maybe it will help me." He wiped his eyes and looked at his daughter. "You were very brave today."

"It is getting easier to be brave. There is nothing else left."

Ahhhh, he thought, while I philosophize, she is becoming philosophical.

"How are we going to get out of here?" he asked in a whisper.

"The Basque shepherd will tell us," she said, pulling the blanket up around his neck. "I am going to help Mama with the meal."

"Where is Samuel?"

"The shepherd is showing him how to sharpen a knife," she said, dropping down from the back of the wagon and walking away.

With the shepherd. And learning to sharpen a knife!

Isaac Bergman's teeth began to chatter, and visions of the German's face swam before his eyes until he finally fell asleep.

"A beer with that, sir?" Perea asked the SS captain after the serving girl had brought the food to his table at the inn.

"If you please," the German said with a smile.

Perea went back to the bar. It was strange. He had never seen any man, much less an SS officer, who smiled so much. And as much as he hated to admit it, it was a nice smile.

He brought the beer and placed it on the table.

"Thank you very much," the captain said, looking at Perea much as a cat looks at a mouse. "Well, do you want me to give you a full report on the investigation now, or would you prefer that I wait and give you a chance to pry it out of me later on?"

"Sir?"

The captain smiled. "Ahhh, I see you want the report now. Very well. The total findings of the investigations —conducted so admirably by the Wehrmacht and the French police—come to exactly nothing."

"They haven't learned anything?"

"Exactly. And from what I observe of their methods, I predict that one week from today they will still know exactly nothing. There, does that make you happy?"

Perea fidgeted with his apron. "Why should that make me happy?"

The German sipped his beer. "I understand the French better than you think. Frenchmen hate to see other Frenchmen punished by anyone who isn't French."

Perea said nothing.

"Let me put your mind at ease. When the saboteurs are captured, they will not be judged and punished by the Germans. We leave that pleasant task to the French authorities. That should be good news to you."

"Oh, yes, sir, that's good news, sir," Perea said, forcing a smile as he walked away.

The Basque entered the dining room while Perea was in the back filling an order. He walked to a small table and sat down. He looked around the room and noticed that the SS captain was having his dinner at the other end of the room. The captain was staring at him. The Basque pretended not to notice and sat patiently, waiting for someone to take his order.

Von Berkow took another sip of his beer. He was annoyed to see the Gypsy, not liking to eat in the same room with one of those dogs. He decided to ignore the man. If he didn't look at him, he could forget he was there.

Perea came out of the back room, looking to see if anyone else required his services. He was startled to see the Basque. He walked over to him.

"Can I get you something?" he asked in a normal tone of voice, and then in a whisper, "What are you doing here?"

"Looking for you."

"There's an SS man over there."

"I know."

"Yes, all right, a beer," Perea said loudly. While he was

getting it, he began to sweat. What does that idiot think this is, a game? Holy Mother of God, he could get us all killed by coming in here!

He brought the beer and the glass and put them down on the Basque's table.

"Where is Renoudot?" Again the whisper.

"Captured."

"Alive?"

"Yes."

Perea was sweating more now. "I must talk with you. Meet me at the back, near the kitchen door. In ten minutes."

"Ten minutes," the Basque said, raising the glass to his lips and taking a sip. He made a face. He didn't like beer. It would have been as easy for Perea to have brought him a glass of wine, he thought. Another reason to dislike him.

The SS captain waved the waiter over to his table. "What does that Gypsy want?" he asked.

"A beer, sir."

The captain looked sharply at him. "Well, I guess that is all right. Even a Gypsy has the right to be thirsty."

Perea walked away and busied himself clearing off tables. Out of the corner of his eye he noticed the Basque leaving.

The SS captain noticed, too. He also noticed the man had barely touched his beer. Again von Berkow had a sense of something being wrong. He puzzled a bit and then gave up and went about eating his dinner.

When Perea came out the back door, the Basque was waiting for him.

"You say Renoudot was captured?"

"Yes. Right before we left Toulouse."

Christ! Perea thought, they will make him talk. "How about the others?" he asked.

"With the Gypsies."

"Why are you with the Gypsies?"

"When the train was blown up, I decided to leave it. Who could tell what would have happened. We took to the road and met the Gypsies. That is all."

"You did the right thing. If you had stayed with the train, you would probably be locked up right now."

"In the church?"

"Yes," Perea said, puzzled. "How did you know about the church?"

"One hears many things on the road."

"We can discuss what has happened some other time. Now that the Germans have captured Renoudot, who knows what they have learned."

"Will he break?"

"Any man can break. We have to assume they will make him talk."

"Maybe they've already done it," the Basque said.

Perea nodded. "We must leave tonight. At three hours after midnight. Everyone will be asleep, and there are few guards at that hour of the morning. I will come to the Gypsy wagons, and everyone should be ready to leave immediately."

"What route will we take?"

"There is a pass in the mountains, and before the pass is a cache where we have hidden supplies and clothing. I will take you to the cache and the pass. From there on it is up to you."

"Which pass is it?"

Perea scratched his head. "I don't know if it has a name. It is a small footpath, not a road."

"Is it the path that goes by the ruins of an old Roman fort?"

"I don't know."

"If it is that one, we are lucky because I know it. It is an old smuggler's path."

"I will ask the proprietor if there are any Roman ruins," Perea said. He paused. "The SS man in the inn hates Gypsies. It is good we are leaving tonight."

The Basque shrugged. Hating Gypsies was nothing new. They didn't have to invent Germans to do that. He thought of another matter. "Renoudot promised I would have another four thousand pesetas."

"What?"

"Yes, four thousand. I did not expect to take four people like these through the mountains."

"What are they like?"

"A thin, weak man. An old woman. A girl. A boy with a crippled leg."

"My God, I didn't know."

"Now you do."

"Is it possible for them to cross?"

"The girl will make it," the Basque said. "And," he added, "the boy, too. He has a bad leg, but his heart is strong, and he has courage."

"The man and the woman?"

"The man I am not sure about. It depends on how much he desires to live. But the woman will never make it."

Perea looked down. "What will we do with her?"

"When she cannot keep up, we will leave her. Those who wish to live will come with me. To linger in the mountains at this time of year is to ask to die."

"We will keep moving."

"And my four thousand pesetas?"

"I will get it for you."

"I want it now."

"I don't have it now. Believe me, if I had it, I would give it to you."

The Basque studied the man. Perhaps he was lying, perhaps not. It didn't matter. He needed Perea because the man knew where the supplies were hidden.

"Three hours after midnight."

"We will be ready," the Basque said.

Perea went back into the inn.

"Where have you been?" the proprietor asked. "We have new customers who are thirsty."

Perea went into the front room. A gendarme growled about his absence.

"One of the serving girls," Perea said with a knowing smile.

The gendarme looked at him for a moment and then broke out into a laugh. "When nature calls a man, that is one thing I never argue with," he said, giving Perea a slap on the back.

When everyone was served, Perea had a moment to stand by the bar and look about the room. The SS captain was still eating, but he had been joined by another officer, a Wehrmacht lieutenant.

Perea had a moment for his thoughts. Renoudot captured. Good God! The worst could happen. Will he break? the Basque had asked. Perea shuddered. It is a good thing the Basque doesn't know what I know about Renoudot. If he did, he would probably be heading for the mountains at this very moment. Once Renoudot had been drunk and had confided in him. He had told about his fear of pain, that he couldn't stand being hurt. He had admitted to being a coward.

What will he do when the Nazis start working him over? The man would probably break down and tell everything.

Perea suddenly gasped.

That SS captain said that he was not here investigating the train wreck, that he was here on another matter.

Another matter?

Perea stared across the room and watched the back of the man's head. What other matter could it be, he said to himself, answering his own question. He is here because Renoudot broke and told them all about Bergman and St. Limoux and the escape and . . . about me!

So why hasn't he arrested any of us?

Because he doesn't know who we are, and he thinks I am a waiter and the others are Gypsies.

But how long will this last?

Not long.

"Here," the proprietor said, interrupting Perea's thoughts. "Bring these two beers to the German officers with my compliments."

Perea took the beers. "Oh, by the way, are there any Roman ruins about?"

"Why do you ask," the proprietor said suspiciously.

"One of the Germans asked me. I didn't know."

The proprietor's suspicions disappeared. "Yes. There is an old fort in the pass off the road from town. The pass splits in two. You take the fork to the right to get to the ruins." He turned and went back to the kitchen.

Perea went over with the beers to where the German officers were having their dinner.

The captain barely glanced up as he put the glasses down.

"I may need your help tomorrow," he was saying to the lieutenant. "I know you were sent here to investigate the train wreck, but something more important has come up."

Perea dared not linger any longer. It did not matter that the SS captain would begin a search in the morning.

It did not matter if the lieutenant's men were detailed to help him.

At three hours after midnight he would be gone from this place. And so would the others.

With the help of God.

12

The first light was breaking.

Born in the cataclysm of fire and lightning, having spent their youth and maturity as an awesome spectacle, the ancient Pyrenees seemed content to slumber as the sun made its appearance at the edge of the earth.

But this was deceptive. The mountains did not sleep. Their infinite power and savagery were there. The heavy boulders threw massive shadows, the shadows often two or three times the size of their maker. Small trees threw long shadows; tall trees threw shadows of trees the size of which have never existed on this earth. There was quiet, a respite from the winds, a moment of silence in a world that could howl like the howls of demons down the corridors of hell. On the higher slopes the ice reflected back the first rays of the sun, the few feeble rays that managed to pierce through the growing mantle of storm cloud. The distant rumbling of thunder reverberated through the canyons and passes and echoed and re-echoed through the jumbled masses of twisted rock until it spent itself.

There was a stillness among the birds. They knew a storm was coming and kept quiet in preparation for the assault, conserving their strength to cope with the titanic power about to be unleashed in their world. A few animals came out to sniff the air, but they, too, sensed what was happening and made their way back to their lairs, by far the best places to weather the storms caused by nature, other animals, or man.

Erno Urquijo filled his lungs with the air. He was a man coming home. He was not very deep in the mountains and not very high, it was true, but he was no longer on the floor of the world, and even here, not very far from all the men and things he hated, he was far enough and deep enough and high enough to know he was back where he belonged.

The clumps of weeds and grasses glistened with the dew.

The trees were kings, their massive feet rooted in the rocky earth, their branches spread like arms reaching out to touch one another. Thick growths of gorse and bracken huddled at the feet of the kings, vassals, men-at-arms, seeking the protection of the outstretched arms.

The curve of the land, for all its meanderings and drops in elevation, caused by the deep gashes that cut through hundreds of tons of rock and the abrupt precipices that fell off suddenly to nothing, for all of this, the curve of the land was upward, forever and inevitably upward.

A hawk soared, a thousand feet up the mountain, spiraling on the paths of the wind, looking for prey, drifting across the sky, a dot.

They had come to a fork in the pass, a narrow canyon bearing off to the left and a narrow canyon bearing off to the right. The Basque was studying the land when Meriam came over to him.

She looked at him for a moment before she spoke. Finally she said, "I saw what you did for my daughter. You are a good man."

The shepherd said nothing. The woman continued, "I want her to live. And my son, too. I want them to live no matter what happens to me, do you understand?"

The Basque nodded his head.

The woman smiled. Their moment of understanding was interrupted by Perea.

"The proprietor of the inn told me about this fork," Perea said. "The Roman ruins are to the right, and it is the easiest way to climb."

"Then we will go to the left," the Basque said. "If anyone is following us, they will assume we would go the easiest way."

Perea nodded. There was nothing wrong with this line of reasoning.

So far everything had gone well. Perea had come to the wagons three hours after midnight, and the six of them had left St. Limoux without being seen by anyone. They had trudged along the road until they came to the first hillock, the beginning of the massive rise in the earth that was the Pyrenees, where Perea had no trouble in finding the hidden cache. There were warm boots, trousers, and heavy coats, climbing equipment, pitons, and food for the journey.

"Look," Perea said proudly, holding up two rifles and a belt of ammunition. "We even thought of these."

When they were dressed, they distributed the packs among the Basque, Perea, and Isaac Bergman, who insisted he should carry his share despite the others' protests. The man winced when the pack was loaded on his back, but he did not complain.

The Basque led the way down the left fork, and within a few hundred feet the path, what there had been of it, disappeared. The Basque stopped. "There are loose rocks. Walk carefully," he said, and continued on.

He had gone a hundred meters when he noticed the others were falling back. He stopped and waited. *The trouble is the woman.* She was being helped along by her daughter and Perea. Meriam would take a few steps, skid on a rock, grab the other two, and stop, looking in agony at the path ahead.

The Basque lit his pipe and waited. He would say nothing for a time. The others must come to see for themselves what he had known before they set foot in the mountains. The woman could not cross. Not in three days. Not in a week. Not in a month. And they did not have a month. Until they crossed to the other side, they were still in French territory. The Germans would pursue them and, at their present pace, no doubt catch them.

He felt something on his cheek. He touched it, and the snowflake melted. He looked up at the sky, and it was heavy with the white powder. He stood there with the tiny flakes dropping on his cap and shoulders until the others finally made their way up to him.

"We must go faster," he said.

No one spoke.

"We will climb down this ledge and make our way along that stream. There is little water in it now. The bed will give us easier footing."

He slid down the ledge and found himself on flat ground about six feet below the others.

Samuel scrambled down with little difficulty and turned to help his father, who almost toppled over backward because of the unaccustomed weight of the pack.

Then it was the mother's turn. Perea and Leah lowered her over the side.

"I'll fall, I'll fall," the woman shrieked.

The Basque regarded the woman. It was not her fault that she was not a mountain climber. But she should also not *try* to be a mountain climber.

"Can we stop for a while?" she asked.

Leah whispered in her ear, and a frightened look came over the woman's face; she began to trudge forward. The Basque turned away and moved along the path.

Perea came up to him. "Do you know where you are going?" he asked.

"Yes. But at this pace it will take weeks."

"Weeks? But when we came from the other side, it only took two days."

"It was a much shorter journey. This is a more difficult part of the mountains. And now there is the snow. It would take long enough if we could keep a good pace, but we are hardly moving. You know the trouble, don't you?"

Perea was silent. He knew, but he did not want to admit it even to himself. They would soon have to make a decision; if they did not, and they were being pursued, they would all be caught.

The Basque looked up at the sky. "This will be a heavy snowfall. The skies are heavy."

"Won't that make it harder for anyone to follow us?"

"Only if it keeps snowing. If it stops, we will leave a trail as clear as the railroad track from Toulouse to St. Limoux."

"Then we should pray it keeps snowing."

"The snow also makes it more difficult to climb."

They followed the stream bed, and the snow continued to fall. The world became silent as the white powder covered the ground and the rocks and the trees.

The Basque and the others moved silently, like ghosts, through a fairyland of grotesque white shapes, enormous monsters that thickened as they turned whiter and whiter in the weak rays of the sun.

Even though they stopped many times during the day, by midafternoon the woman was exhausted. The Basque invented an excuse to halt.

"I'm hungry," he said, taking the pack off his back.

Leah opened her father's pack and began to pass out frozen pieces of bread and cheese. She opened one package and looked curiously at the contents. "What is this?" she asked the Basque.

He looked at it. "Eel."

"Eel!" she said with a look of distaste.

"Chew it slowly. It will give you strength."

"But eel! I've never eaten eel before."

"And you have never climbed through mountains before," he said.

She nibbled at the end and chewed it. "It doesn't taste like anything."

"Because it is frozen."

She took another small bite. "I'm glad. This way I can't taste it." She chewed for a few moments, then turned to the Basque. "Mama is slowing us down, isn't she?"

The Basque said nothing.

"I know she is," the girl said. "I'm surprised you haven't said anything."

"Tonight I will say what I must say."

Leah shuddered. She looked over at her mother, who was too exhausted to touch the bread and cheese on her lap. "I must help my mother," she said.

The Basque took another swig of wine from his *chahakoa.* The wine had been in a jar with the supplies, and he had transferred it to his wineskin. Good wine, he thought. These people thought of everything. Well, not everything; they did not remember that winter is a bad time for a woman like this one to be in the mountains.

They resumed their journey. The path became steeper. Perea and the girl had more and more difficulty with Meriam. She stumbled over the smallest rock and slipped on the snow. She wore heavy boots, but they did not do much good. She would stop every few steps and gasp for air. Her husband tried to help her, but he only got in the way, and finally Perea ordered him on ahead.

The sun was disappearing behind the peak of a mountain when the Basque began looking for a large, fallen tree, one large enough to camp under. He finally saw what he was looking for and stopped. "This is where we will spend the night."

Samuel came to his side. "Why here?"

"The branches will protect us from the snow and the wind." We can even have a fire."

"Isn't that dangerous?" Samuel asked. "What if someone sees it?"

"I do not think there will be anyone to see it. Tomorrow may be different, but tonight we will be brave and enjoy one last fire."

They cleared a path that led under the tree where the frozen ground was mostly free of snow. The branches of the tree above were filled with snow and formed a protective canopy. The Basque and Samuel began to collect twigs and small sticks. "Pick the ones which are dry," the Basque said.

The fire was small, but it gave off some warmth, and the group huddled in gratitude about it. They heated water, and Perea made tea. They placed food by the fire, and after it thawed, they ate hungrily, greedily, without talking. Again, Meriam made no attempt to eat.

The Basque lit his pipe and puffed a big cloud of smoke toward the fire.

"I have something to say."

They all turned to him except Meriam, who continued to stare at the fire.

"We have spent one day in the mountains. Perhaps the easiest day."

Isaac Bergman closed his eyes. God help us, he thought.

"The ground has not been very difficult. And the snow has not had a chance to drift. Tomorrow will be different. The climb becomes steeper. There is one ridge we must cross where there are no paths. After that there is a long ravine we must follow, and then we have a long climb up a high ridge. When we have climbed that ridge and have gone down the other side, we will be in Spain."

The boy clapped his hands but stopped quickly when the Basque stared at him.

"The time to cheer is when we are on the other side. We are not on the other side."

"I'm sorry."

"At the pace we kept today, it will take us at least a week."

"A week!" Leah said in horror. "A week and we'll still be on the French side of the mountains?"

"Yes."

The Bergmans stared at the ground. No one dared look at anyone else. A week! A week with enough supplies only for a few days. A week on this cold rock with the powdery white death falling on them all day long. A week that would stretch out hour by hour until it became a time too long for the body to endure.

"In the morning," the Basque said, "I will set the pace.

If you stay with me, I will show you the way through the mountains. If you do not, I will leave you behind."

"But you promised to guide these people through the mountains," Perea said. "You have been well paid."

"Not well enough to die."

"He is right," Samuel said. There was a stubborn look on his face. He has made his decision, the Basque thought. When I start out tomorrow, this one will stay with me. He wants to live, and when the will to live is strong, everything that threatens life is rejected. He looked over and saw Bergman staring at his son.

"Go to sleep," the Basque said. "You need strength for tomorrow." He rested his back against a branch. The others curled up near the fire. The two older Bergmans sat together, their eyes open. They did not talk.

The snow fell steadily on the frozen earth.

13

Gunther von Berkow was in the church watching them beat a man. The Wehrmacht lieutenant had decided to follow the captain's advice and get tougher with the suspects.

The light was dim and murky through the narrow windows. Several men were seated in an alcove, guarded by a soldier with a rifle. At the front of the church there was a table set near the altar rail. Von Berkow and the lieutenant sat at the table while a burly soldier worked on the suspect, who had fallen to his knees.

"Why did you blow up the train?" the burly soldier asked the bleeding Frenchman for the twentieth time.

"I did not do it," the man sputtered through broken teeth.

The piece of rubber hose crashed into the man's ear, bringing forth another scream.

The Wehrmacht lieutenant turned to von Berkow. "This doesn't seem to be getting us anywhere."

"Maybe you are questioning the wrong people?"

The lieutenant looked puzzled.

"Perhaps you haven't captured any of the saboteurs," von Berkow explained.

"But how is one to know which are the saboteurs?"

"After a time you develop an *instinct.*"

The lieutenant shook his head. "I am not comfortable doing this sort of work."

"Then stop doing it."

"But you are the one who suggested this method of questioning in the first place," the lieutenant protested.

"Lieutenant, you have to torture someone who knows something in the first place. If they don't know anything, they can't tell you anything."

"And this one?" the lieutenant said, indicating the bleeding Frenchman.

"My instinct tells me he knows nothing."

"Let him go," the lieutenant said to the soldier who had been using the rubber hose.

As the soldier untied the dazed Frenchman and pushed him toward the door, Captain von Berkow put on his cap. "I am going to get some dinner at the inn. Do you care to join me?"

The two Germans left the church and walked down the street. Von Berkow looked at the buildings and admired the carvings under the eaves of many of the houses. Many of the images were of animals: dogs, rams, and bulls. They had been well carved and, from their weather-beaten appearance, had been looking out on the street of St. Limoux for more than two or three hundred years. Some of the houses bore crests and coats of arms with a form of swastika on them. A peculiar curvilinear swastika that had been part of the Basque decorative art for untold centuries.

"Notice the swastikas?" von Berkow asked his companion.

"They seem to be everywhere."

"Which proves these people have been good National Socialists for centuries. Long before the Germans, in fact." He said this without the trace of a smile.

The lieutenant looked at him sharply. He did not wish to agree or disagree with such a preposterous statement. He wasn't sure about this captain's sense of humor.

"On the other hand, these swastikas might signify man's subconscious urge to be a National Socialist, even though there was no such thing when these crests were carved."

The lieutenant realized the captain was making sport with him. "Yes, that could be true," he said.

They entered the inn and took a table near the window. Two Frenchmen, who had been seated at the next table, got up and quickly left the inn.

"We seem to be unpopular," the lieutenant said.

Von Berkow turned back to his companion. "Unpopular? Yes, we are unpopular with the French because they think we have taken their country. But what right do they have to this place? They are Gauls who took it from the Celts. The Celts, in turn, took the British Isles from the Britons. The Angles and the Saxons, who are Germans, took Britain from the Celts. The Normans, who are French, took Britain from the Angles and the Saxons. And now the Saxons, which is what we are, if you will, are taking France back from the Normans. But who of all these people has a right to any of it? Who has a right to claim a country except by right of arms?"

The lieutenant looked very surprised.

"Something the matter with my logic?" von Berkow asked.

The lieutenant was embarrassed. "No, it's not that. It's, well, I didn't expect you to be a scholar."

"My dear lieutenant," Von Berkow said dryly, "we of the SS are the scholars of our times."

The proprietor came over with two beers.

Von Berkow took a sip, and a thought occurred to him. "Who are you?" he said.

"Sir? Why, I am the owner of this inn."

"I see," von Berkow said thoughtfully. "Where is the other waiter?"

"The other waiter, sir?"

"The one who was here yesterday?"

"I don't know. He never showed up today. I don't know where he is."

"What is his name?"

The proprietor scratched his head. "He never told me. I don't know his name."

"A man works for you, and you don't know his name?"

"He worked here for only two days. He hasn't even come for his pay."

Von Berkow's voice dropped to a whisper. "You say he worked here for only two days?"

"Yes."

"Did you know him before he worked here?"

"No."

"Was he from the town?"

"I never saw him before."

Damn it! A waiter who shows up from nowhere exactly at the time of a train wreck and then disappears without picking up his pay. Von Berkow's mind was working rapidly. He had already decided that if Bergman was coming to St. Limoux, he was probably planning to escape through the mountains. There would, no doubt, be people waiting here for him.

"Did the man act suspicious? Do or say anything strange?"

"No, I can't remember him saying . . . oh, well, yes, one time he asked me a question about the Roman fort in the pass up in the mountains. It seems like a strange time of year to go into the mountains."

Captain von Berkow waved the man away and sat lost in thought, trying to piece the puzzle together. The Wehrmacht lieutenant did not want to interrupt and sat staring out the window, watching the Gypsies. After a while von Berkow followed his gaze, and suddenly it was as if the key to a jigsaw had fallen into place.

The Gypsies.

The waiter.

The old sick Gypsy with the puny hand.

He had held the hand of Isaac Bergman!

"Damn!" he shouted. The lieutenant jumped up, astonished. The proprietor shrank back, awaiting God knows what from this SS devil.

"Bring a detail of men to the Gypsy wagons," von Berkow said to the lieutenant.

The captain threw some francs on the table and walked out, leaving a bewildered proprietor regarding the money. It was far too much. He shrugged. All Germans were strange. It is a good thing this one does not know I fought in the last war, he thought. A hero with a medal. They would either laugh about it or shoot me. Germans are that unpredictable.

Von Berkow arrived at the wagons at the same time as the lieutenant, who had a half-dozen soldiers at his heels.

The Gypsies looked up and then away. The women continued preparing their meal until the captain kicked the heavy cooking pot off the fire. The women stared at him, their faces without expression.

"All Gypsies out!"

The soldiers moved quickly among the people, shouting, *"Raus, raus,"* moving them from the wagons. They used their rifle butts to line them up. Von Berkow passed down the line, peering into each face.

Where was the sickly old man? Where was his daughter, the pretty one named Marie? "Is this is all of them?" he asked the lieutenant.

"Yes, sir."

Von Berkow walked up to the leader. It was cold, but the fat man was sweating. Another face was missing.

"Where is your brother?"

The fat Gypsy's eyes bulged. "My . . . brother?"

"The one who sat beside you when you arrived."

"Oh."

"Where is he?"

"Who, sir?"

Von Berkow restrained himself. "Your brother."

"My brother?"

"Yes."

"I . . . do not know."

"He isn't your brother, is he?" Pleasantly.

"Sir . . . I . . . he . . ." The Gypsy stopped. His lips moved silently.

"He isn't your brother, is he?"

The Gypsy was in a state of terror beyond speech.

"Who was that man? And who was the old man who was sick? And his daughter? Who were those people?" von Berkow asked in a very low voice.

No answer.

The captain smiled. He put on his gloves and slipped

his SS dagger from the sheath on his belt. "One more chance, Gypsy. I have no time for games. Who are those people, and where are they?"

Silence.

"I will be very direct, Gypsy."

Silence.

"Hold him," he said to the soldiers. Two of them grabbed the fat Gypsy from each side.

"On his knees."

The soldiers forced the Gypsy down on his knees in front of the captain. The man started to blubber, and flecks of spittle ran over his lips and down his chin. Von Berkow grabbed the man by the hair and held his head back. In his right hand he twisted his SS dagger so the hilt was pointing toward the Gypsy. He jammed the end of the dagger with great force into the Gypsy's left eye. He kept grinding and pushing until thick, viscous liquids began to stream over the end of the hilt. The fluids were mixed with blood.

There was a scream.

There are screams of fear and screams of warning and screams of pain.

And there are screams.

The man's eyeball burst on the end of the knife, and he screamed, and it was such a scream that people who were talking stopped; and people who were walking stopped; and the town stopped. They froze and listened to the scream, and it was not the scream of a human being. Human lungs could not bring forth the notes of such agony.

Von Berkow pulled the dagger away and gazed into the white face of the one-eyed Gypsy. There were fluids and blood and bits of flesh on the end of the dagger.

"Who are those people?"

The Gypsy moved his lips, but no words emerged, no

human sounds, more the terrified bleating of an animal under the knife. And then he coughed blood.

"You have another eye, Gypsy."

The Wehrmacht lieutenant was looking on with horror. He had never seen anything like this in his life. It was not even in his lexicon of horror. He could not believe it happened even though he had seen it for himself.

The other Gypsies were straining to look. There was a terror among them so real it had a *presence*. You could see it and feel it and almost touch it. The man next to the fat Gypsy, who had seen everything, passed out. Women began to cry, but the rifle butts of the soldiers forced them to be quiet.

"I will tell," the fat Gypsy said, barely whispering.

Von Berkow bent down and put his ear near the man's mouth. "Where are they?"

"I do not know. They were gone when we woke this morning."

"All of them."

"Yes."

"How many?"

"The family and the guide."

"How many in the family?"

"Four. The couple. Two children. Boy and girl." The blood dripped down from his eye, around the bridge of his nose, and into his mouth.

Four, Von Berkow thought. That agreed with the information he had gotten from Renoudot. "The sick old man," he said, "he is the father?"

"Yes."

"He is not a Gypsy?"

"No."

"And the guide? Is he the one who said he was your brother?"

"Yes."

"Where did they come from?"

"I do not know."

"Gypsy, remember the other eye."

"Please. We met them on the road. I do not know where they were coming from. They paid me money to bring them to St. Limoux."

"Who is the guide?"

"A Basque; other than that I do not know. He told me he was being paid to bring the others to St. Limoux. He talked very little."

"Who paid him?"

The Gypsy tried to answer but began to cough and could not stop. Blood and saliva trickled down his chin and neck into his shirt. The blood flowed freely from the mangled eye socket.

Captain von Berkow stood up.

Bergman had been here, and now he was gone, probably with the waiter from the inn.

Von Berkow looked at the mountains, then back toward the fat Gypsy. "Shoot him," he said to the Wehrmacht lieutenant, turning and walking toward the guardhouse.

The fat Gypsy was dragged over to a wall and propped up in a sitting position. The crying and sobbing Gypsies huddled together near the first wagon. Six soldiers lined up in front of the wall, their rifles pointed toward the victim. The order was given, and six bullets pounded into the man's body. He fell over on the ground, his body torn and shabby, a mound of dead flesh. His pain was done.

The acrid smell of gunpowder wafted through the town. Doors were shut as people scurried inside. Window shutters were closed. Nothing moved. St. Limoux was a place of fear.

The lieutenant returned to the guardhouse where Captain von Berkow snapped out his orders. He needed a small party of men and a French guide. They were going into the mountains at dawn.

Meriam Bergman watched the fire burn lower. There was still heat from the glowing embers. She shivered. The embers did no good. The fire did no good. Nothing did any good. She would never be warm again in her life.

I am going to die.

The thought kept repeating itself in her head. It was impossible for her to live through another day like this one. Each step had become more and more of an agony. She had only come this far out of fear that the Basque would leave them to die.

She could feel her muscles stiffening. By morning she would be in such pain she doubted if she would be able to walk at all.

Before he had gone to sleep, her husband had tried to comfort her. "Don't worry, Meriam, everything is going to be all right."

Yes, yes, leave it to him not to face the truth.

"Tomorrow we will go nice and slow," he said. "I will speak to the shepherd. He will understand."

Fool, he will understand nothing. She looked curiously at her husband. Always she had been his dutiful servant. Always she had agreed with him and had done what he wanted. And now? I am tired of agreeing with him. I am tired of doing what he wants. Why did he always assume he knew more than I did? Why was he the one who made all the decisions?

She wanted to say this but kept still. It is my last night on earth, she thought. Why should I stick a knife in his heart now?

"We have had a good life together, have we not?" he said.

She stared at the fire. Good? What is good? It had been a comfortable life, an easy life. And we had the children. Two wonderful children who revolved about her like twin moons around Mother Earth. Or, at least, had revolved about her. Leah was grown up, with a mind of her own.

"Samuel is a fine lad," Isaac Bergman said.

Her only son. He, too, was leaving the nest. It had happened so suddenly. Only yesterday, it seemed, he was still her "little boy" coming home from school, drinking his milk and eating a piece of pastry. But this experience had changed him. All day long I struggled and battled with the snow, and hardly ever did he come and help me. But I am finished with blaming others for my unhappiness. I am finished with sighing and accepting quietly what I did not want to accept. If I cannot be honest with myself now, when will I ever be?

"Don't you feel like talking?" Isaac asked.

She looked at him, and he was a stranger.

"Are you too tired to talk?" he persisted.

"There is nothing to say," she said.

"After all these years," he said, "it breaks my heart to see you suffering like this. Can I get anything for you?"

"Nothing."

"Here, put this pack behind you. It makes a pillow," he said, shifting his pack and propping it behind her. "You'll sleep better. You heard what the shepherd said. We have a long day ahead of us tomorrow, and we should sleep to build up our strength."

Strength. She had none left, and a night's sleep would do no good. If she fell asleep, her muscles would stiffen and harden; that was all she would get from a night's sleep.

And who wants to sleep on their last night on earth?

She had said these words to herself several times now, and she realized they were the truth. She shuddered. She looked at her husband for a long time. "Isaac, tell me, do you think I have been a good wife?"

The question surprised him. "Of course, of course you've been a good wife."

"And a good mother?"

"Yes, a wonderful mother. The children love you."

"And a good person?"

"Good person? Yes. A good mother and a good wife. That makes you a good person."

"Thank you, Isaac," she said with a little smile. "Go to sleep now. It will be a long day tomorrow."

"You go to sleep, too."

"Yes."

He rolled over on his side, and his eyes closed. In the flickering light of the hot embers, she saw his breathing grow heavier, and she knew he was asleep. Poor Isaac. He wasn't used to climbing mountains, either.

But he has a chance to get through and live. I do not.

At last, at long last I am facing life and seeing the truth, and I know what must be done. As long as I am alive to stumble and fall on the trail, my husband and my daughter will not leave me. She smiled. My son is the only one here with sense. He will go with the shepherd. He knows he cannot help me. He knows I want him to live.

But the other two will stay with me. And die with me. All for what? They cannot die for me. I am already dead. They can do nothing for me. I must make their decision for them. They cannot stay with me if I am not here to stay with.

She looked at the others. They were all asleep.

She rolled away from the fire, raised herself up on her hands and knees, and crawled toward the little entrance. When she reached it, she turned and took one last look at her children.

One person watched her go. The Basque. The sound of her heavy coat brushing on the branches brought him out of his light sleep. He watched through half-lidded eyes. He did not move. When she was gone, he dropped back into sleep.

It was freezing cold. The snow continued to fall, and there was no moon. She could see a few feet before her. She continued on all fours through the powder until she came to a flat piece of ground. Then she stood up and began to walk. She didn't know where she got the strength to keep going. Her hands and face were starting to freeze, her feet becoming numb. She stumbled and fell in the snow. It was so good to lie down. But no! It was too soon. She dragged her body up off the ground, holding on to the edge of a sharp ledge that protruded from the mountain. Her hands were torn as the razor edges of the rock cut into her palms.

More steps. More agony. Finally the pain grew until there was a haze before her eyes. She had gone far enough. And if she hadn't, it didn't matter because she could walk no more. She dropped to her hands and knees and crawled the last few feet into the trees.

She reached the first tree and crawled to the base of the trunk. She leaned her back against the icy wood, crusted with frozen lichen. The thick branches, six feet above her head, kept the snow from falling directly on her, but she was still exposed, and the wind swirled the snow through the air and deposited a fine powder on the length of her body.

She had done it.

They would not miss her until the morning. By then it would be too late. They would go on without her. Her daughter and her son would go on to live.

She no longer felt the cold.

She felt warmer, much warmer.

She tried to wiggle her toes in the heavy boots. The toes felt warm and toasty. Even her face felt warmer.

It's all right, it's all right, she told herself. My family is safe, and now you are starting to feel warmer. Everything will be all right. She didn't notice the snowflakes that had fallen on her cheek. The feeble warmth from her body caused them to melt and run down to her collar where they turned to ice. She closed her eyes. Snowflakes fell on the eyelids. They melted and turned to ice as more snowflakes fell.

Her head nodded on her chest.

It was nice to be warm again. So nice.

She nodded once or twice and then fell into a deep sleep.

The snow continued to drift, and the heat went from her body.

She was peacefully asleep as she froze to death.

14

Gunther von Berkow stood by the side of the truck, a handsome figure in his white uniform. White coat, white trousers, white hat. His pistol and dagger were strapped to the white leather belt, which had a thinner piece of leather running up across his chest and over his shoulder. He carried a small pack on his back and a high-powered rifle in his hand.

The Wehrmacht lieutenant came from the guard-house, followed by four yawning soldiers who carried packs and rifles. The French gendarme was already sitting in the middle seat of the cab of the truck.

"We are ready," the lieutenant said, climbing into the back of the truck.

Captain von Berkow climbed into the cab and closed the door.

The driver released the brake, and with a great

amount of squealing and grinding, the truck moved off into the blackness of the predawn.

"We will drive as far as we can," the Frenchman said. "After that we will walk. The path is easy at first, and we will be able to move in the dark. When it starts to get difficult, the sun will be coming up."

"They have a full day's start on us."

"You said there was a woman and children. We should have no trouble making up the time."

Good, von Berkow thought. He wanted to capture Bergman alive and personally hand him over to the Reichsführer. It could mean his next promotion. He stared out into the darkness, a smile turning up the corners of his mouth.

The road dwindled from an ordinary dirt road to a path to a sloping hill strewn with rock. Finally the driver stopped beside a boulder, disengaged the gear, and pulled the brake handle.

"This is as far as this old bird will go," he said.

Von Berkow stepped to the ground as the men tumbled out of the back.

It was dark, but a darkness tempered by a lighter haze, which preceded the appearance of the day. The rain that fell was beginning to turn to snow. The soldiers stomped their feet and rubbed their hands together. It was bitter cold, and they grumbled among themselves. They had been happy when they had been sent to France, delighted with the prospects of French women, French wine, and the pleasures of Paris. So what were they doing here, at the base of a mountain range, preparing to go on a manhunt in the snow?

The gendarme walked around the boulder and the party of seven walked off, leaving the driver and his truck. He watched until he couldn't see them anymore, then climbed into the truck and returned to St. Limoux.

The Frenchman and the soldiers were dressed in dark clothing and appeared, from a distance, as moving shadows against a field of white. There was a longer space between the first and third shadows. Until you got much closer, you could not see that there was another man—another shadow—in that space. It was a white shadow. Gunther von Berkow.

The soldiers labored as they climbed, but the captain moved easily over the rough path.

They came to a fork.

Von Berkow examined the trails leading from the fork. Both were covered with new snow.

"Which way?" he asked the guide.

"The Roman fort is to the right."

"Can we be sure they went that way?"

"The path is easier," the Frenchman said. "It is also the shorter way through the mountains."

Von Berkow studied the land. "What happens to these two paths?" he said to the Frenchman. "Do they come back together and meet each other somewhere in the mountains?"

"No. The one on the right bends toward the west and comes out about twenty miles from the one on the left. They never meet."

"We will go to the right," the captain said.

The guide nodded and started up the path to the right.

Gunther Von Berkow followed, but he was troubled. He looked back on the path to the left. All logic told him they should take the path to the right. Yet . . . there was something wrong.

He had a feeling he had made the wrong choice.

*   *   *

It was dark when the Basque awoke. The fire had died, and the chill of night invaded the cave of branches. He took a piece of cheese from his pack and began chewing it.

The others stirred. Perea stood up and waved his arms. "Damn, it's cold."

Leah woke and rubbed her eyes. She looked around and was concerned. "Where is Mama?"

Samuel was awake instantly. "I don't know," he said.

"She may be outside," Perea said.

"What would she be doing outside?" Leah said, but she went to the entrance and crawled between the snow-covered branches.

The Basque said nothing.

Isaac Bergman woke up. "Good morning, good morning," he said, trying to put some cheer in his voice.

"Leah is outside looking for Mama," Samuel said.

"Outside?"

The girl came back. "I didn't see her anywhere."

The Basque moved to the entrance. "Everyone should eat some cheese and bread."

"But where is my wife?"

The Basque went outside, and the others followed, still not understanding what had happened.

"We must look for Mama," the girl said.

"How do you suggest we find her?" the Basque asked.

"We will just . . . spread out and look around," Leah said.

"We will lose time," the Basque said.

"But she may be freezing," Bergman said. "She may need us at this very moment."

"Why did she come out here alone in the first place?" Samuel asked, looking at the shepherd.

"The reason is unimportant," the Basque said. "She went out last night, and there is no use looking for her now."

"Why not?" Bergman asked.

The Basque looked at him but said nothing. He did not need to say anything.

Suddenly Bergman's confusion turned to understanding and then to anger. "You saw her leave?" When the Basque made no response, Bergman's voice rose. "And you let her go?" He paused to fill his lungs with air. "You let her go out to die?"

His face contorted, and his son and daughter looked at him in surprise. This was a person they had never seen. Suddenly Bergman threw himself at the Basque, flailing wildly with his arms, shouting, "I will kill you!"

The Basque easily pushed him away. Bergman stumbled and fell. He picked himself up and tried to swing at the other man. This time the Basque grabbed him and spun him around. Perea grabbed Bergman and pinned his arms. Gently but forcefully he led him away from the shepherd. He made the professor sit down on a snow-covered boulder. The man immediately placed his face in his hands and wept.

His son looked at him and was confused.

"We must go," the Basque said.

"Not until we look for Mama," the girl said. There was determination in her voice, strength. "I will not leave without trying to find her."

The boy looked at the Basque. He wanted to please the shepherd, but even so, the woman was his mother, and he had never heard his sister use a tone of voice like this. He didn't think he had the strength of will to argue with her.

"Let the dead bury themselves," the Basque said.

Tears came to the girl's eyes. She started to speak but did not.

"Can't we look?" Samuel asked the Basque, his eyes pleading. "Only for a short while. If we don't find her, we will go on."

The Basque gave in. "Listen to me," he said. "We will look for half an hour. No more. It is a waste of time, but if you must, you must." He walked down the path they had trod the day before. "I will go this way," he said.

He shook his head. The woman went out to die. Why don't we leave her alone and let her get what she wants?

He walked for less than ten minutes when he saw her, propped up against a tree. There was no protection in this place, and she had probably frozen quickly. He stood over the form and brushed away the snow. The woman had been granted her wish. She was no longer a burden to her family. They could now go on and live.

"Hola!" the Basque called.

"Hola!" It was the voice of Perea, from a distance.

"I have found her!"

They came and stared at the body. The girl was first. For a full minute Bergman was silent. Finally he spoke, his voice barely a whisper. "Why?"

"To save us," Leah said.

Bergman looked at his daughter, not comprehending.

"She knew we would not leave her," the girl said. "She did not want to be a burden."

"But she was not a burden," he protested.

The others said nothing.

"We must bury her," Bergman said after a long silence.

"No," the Basque said angrily.

Leah was about to speak, but one look at the Basque's face silenced her.

"She was a brave woman," he said. "She went out to die by herself because she knew she could not make it through the mountains. She did not want you to stay with her and die with her."

They stared at the frozen body, the icy flesh that had once been Meriam Bergman.

"We have no shovels to dig," the Basque said. "And if we did, it would take hours in this frozen ground. The woman died to save you. We must go on."

The Bergman family stared at the woman.

Perea coughed. "We will cover her with snow. That will take only a minute," he said, and began scooping up the white powder with his hands and dropping it on the body.

"Stop that," Bergman said.

Perea stopped and looked at the Basque. Before either of them said anything, the girl began to scoop snow on the body of her mother. Samuel watched for a moment, and then he began to scoop snow with his bare hands. In a few minutes the body had disappeared. Bergman stood to the side. He said nothing.

They went back to their cave of branches and shouldered their packs. The Basque divided the contents of Bergman's between his own and Perea's, and Bergman made no protest. The group moved away from the fallen tree.

The footpaths were treacherous, the snow loose and slippery. The falling snow covered them with a fine powder, and they became white specks blending into the whiteness about them. There was glare even though the heavy cloud cover did not let the sun through.

They passed down a ravine, and the boy stumbled several times.

They came to a huge rock that filled the narrow ravine. The snow had gathered about the rock and was waist high. The Basque used his climbing axe to grip an exposed face of the rock as he dragged himself over the snow to the top. He anchored his feet and leaned over, offering the end of the axe to the girl. She grasped it and pulled herself up. The boy followed with little difficulty. Bergman was a problem. After wasting ten minutes,

Perea solved the problem by getting behind Bergman and shoving him up far enough for the Basque to reach down and grab the man's hands and pull him up.

They passed over the side of a hill. There were few trees, and the cold was intense. The wind slashed through their clothes and pricked their skin. When they crossed the hill, they entered a thin grove of conifers. The trees broke the force of the wind and kept the snow from falling on them.

"A short rest," the Basque announced. They sat on the ground, leaning against the trees, exhausted.

"Can we build a fire?" the boy asked.

"There is not enough time," the Basque said.

The boy nodded and opened his pocket and took out a piece of cheese. "I'm sorry Mama had to die," he said.

"She was a brave woman."

"And you were right in not letting us bury her."

The Basque lit his pipe and smoked. This was not the same boy he had first met in Toulouse.

After the brief rest they spent the afternoon clawing and panting their way up the ravine. Each step was a peril. Beneath the soft snow there lay a tangle of roots and loose rocks. It would be easy to get caught in the cleft of two rocks and break a leg. A broken leg here would have the same effect as a bullet in the brain.

The five ghosts moved silently, slowly. They became dwarfed as the dimensions of their surroundings grew larger. The rocks became boulders, and the boulders became miniature mountains, pieces of obstruction thrown from the tops of mountains to block their way. The mountain was putting forth its challenge, and the five people endured it.

15

Gunther von Berkow stood with his foot on a block of stone that had once been a part of the wall of the Roman fort.

An outpost of the conquerors of the world. A reminder that the might of Rome had been here, extending from the Delta of the Nile to the Bosporus to the Pillars of Hercules to the fringes of the lands of the Britons and Teutonic tribes that dwelt in the northern forests.

The stones of the fort were strong, but the centuries and the various armies and migrations of Vandals, Goths, Alemanni, Huns, Ostrogoths, Suevi, and later the Saxons and the Franks and the Lombards and the Normans and the French, all had taken their toll, and the fort lay empty, a dead thing. A pile of mildewed stone, turning white under the falling snow, a tribute to man's ambition, which built monuments, only to see them destroyed by the vanity of time.

The captain was troubled.

They were following the path Bergman was *supposed* to be taking. All logic dictated it. But what if he was not doing what he was *supposed* to be doing? The captain had a strange feeling about that Basque guide who was with Bergman. The fellow was crafty. He disguised himself and the others as Gypsies and escaped from right under my nose, von Berkow thought. It also appeared that Bergman and the Basque had been on the sabotaged train. His first thought had been that they had something to do with the explosion, but he had dismissed this as ridiculous.

That damned Basque guide! If I were he, von Berkow thought, I would expect us to be acting exactly the way we are acting. The Basque would assume we are thinking the way we are thinking. We expect him to go the easiest way. He knows that, so what would he do?

What would I do?

I would go the other way, the way I was not expected to go, the path to the left.

We have taken the wrong path. It was not a guess. He knew it to be a fact.

He growled. It had taken them three hours to get to the fort. Assuming they turned around immediately and went up the left fork, they had lost a minimum of six hours. He muttered under his breath.

The French gendarme had been prowling around, looking for footprints. He came over to von Berkow.

"Did you find anything?"

"Nothing," the Frenchman said with a shrug. "But with all this fresh snow . . ." He shrugged again. "If they passed by here more than an hour ago, there would be nothing left to see."

"If we follow this path and come out on the other side, can we turn east and come to the head of the other fork?"

"Yes."

"Would that be quicker than turning back and following the other fork from here?"

"The two forks come out at great distances from one another on the other side. It would be quicker to turn around here."

Von Berkow made his decision. "We are going back and taking the other fork."

"Why?"

Von Berkow ignored him and went over to the German soldiers, who were huddled together, smoking cigarettes, stomping their feet.

"We are going back to take the other fork," he said to the lieutenant.

"You have found something?" the lieutenant asked.

"It is the way our prey has gone. Don't ask stupid questions," von Berkow said.

The lieutenant looked sharply at him. Is that the way the captain thought of these people? *Prey.* The lieutenant was uncomfortable. There was something about this captain, something savage and inhuman. He remembered the fat Gypsy's eye and shuddered. The man had ripped out the eye and squashed it like a grape.

"If we turn back and start up the path in the other direction, we will already have lost several hours," the French gendarme said. "If the other path is the wrong path . . ."

The captain understood. If the left fork was wrong, and they doubled back and spent even a full day in that direction, they could never come back this way and hope to catch up to Bergman. The man would be lost forever.

But something inside told him it was the right decision. Bergman had taken the path to the left. He was sure of it.

"We take the other fork," he said.

They did not argue with him. The Frenchman shrugged. The soldiers, who overheard everything, looked at one another. What the hell was going on? Didn't they just come up this path, and now they were turning back. One raised his arm in a gesture of futility. Another put his finger to the side of his head and made a circular motion. The others chuckled and nodded. It was easy to understand. Simply a case of another crazy officer.

The Frenchman went first, and the captain was at his heels. "Faster," he hissed.

"It is bad footing and . . ."

"I didn't ask for talk. Go faster," the captain said, cutting him off.

The Frenchman nodded unhappily and moved faster over the snow-covered rock. The others picked up the pace. The soldiers grumbled. But they did not grumble loudly enough for it to reach the captain.

They arrived at the fork, and the captain drove the men on through the day, not bothering to stop for a rest or a break to eat. The Frenchman complained at one point, but the captain told him to shut up or he would put a bullet in his brain. He said it very pleasantly, even smiling as he said it.

The terrified Frenchman maintained the rapid pace. He kept it up until late afternoon.

As they approached a ridge and passed a clump of trees, the captain stopped suddenly. He gazed at a large fallen tree off to the left. He walked through the drifts until he came near the fallen giant. There were other, smaller trees that grew along the length of their big brother. He walked under one of these smaller trees.

He saw the remains of footprints, almost obliterated but still visible, protected through the day by the branches of the tree. He walked farther along the trunk of the fallen giant until he saw what appeared to be a small opening that led under the trunk. He squirmed through the hole. It was dark under the tree, but not so dark that he couldn't see. In the middle of the space were the remains of a fire. He picked up some of the charred remains and put them to his nose. A recent fire.

He came back outside. "Bergman spent the night here," he said to the lieutenant, his eyes blazing with triumph. "I was right. They did come this way."

"On your feet," he said to the French gendarme, who had slumped down on top of a rock.

"But, my Captain," the weary man said, "it is getting dark. It is dangerous to move at night. Besides, everyone is exhausted. We should rest and eat."

"We will move forward," von Berkow said. "They are a full day ahead of us, a full day! I want to make up some of that time."

"But we are moving faster than these people."

"Get up!"

The Frenchman and the soldiers groaned, but they got to their feet.

The Frenchman led the way. They moved forward quickly, von Berkow muttering and pushing the Frenchman, who was terrified at traveling over rough terrain at night, but even more terrified of the man who walked at his shoulder.

"We must make up time," the SS man kept saying. "They must not get too far ahead of us."

It finally happened. Men should not move so swiftly up the face of a mountain in a snowstorm and in the dark.

There was a scream from the next to last soldier as his

foot caught in an unseen hole between two rocks. His momentum and the heavy pack on his back forced him forward. *Craaaack!* The soldier was shouting and screaming.

Von Berkow and the lieutenant came back to the man, and the others gathered around. The lieutenant tried to inspect the leg, but the man screamed when it was touched.

"The leg is broken," the lieutenant said.

"Badly?"

"Yes."

Von Berkow was annoyed. "Find a place for this man to spend the night," he said to the Frenchman. "As close to here as possible."

The men found a thick grove of trees about thirty meters away. They carried the soldier with the broken leg, who grunted and moaned and once, when they stumbled and almost dropped him, screamed because the break was a bad one, the bone jutting out through the skin, causing great pain.

They rested in the trees. The haggard faces of the men showed their relief at being out of the wind and snow and being able to relax. In minutes they had a cheery fire going. The lieutenant tended to the man, making a splint for the leg, giving him painkilling pills. Another soldier heated soup and fed it to him.

"He must start back down in the morning. That break is a bad one. It will become infected," the lieutenant said to von Berkow as the two of them drank soup from metal cups. The cups were hot and burned their hands, but it was good.

"Not much chance of infection in this cold."

"He must go back. As soon as possible. Daybreak."

"Agreed."

"Hegel will stay behind and help him."

"Who is Hegel?"

"One of the soldiers."

Von Berkow's eyes narrowed. "You are cutting our forces in half?"

The lieutenant shrugged. "What can I do? The man cannot make it down by himself. God knows it will be difficult enough with only one to help him."

"I cannot allow you to reduce our forces," von Berkow said.

"What do you suggest? That we leave the man alone?"

"Why not?"

"He will die."

"If that happens, it happens. The man is a soldier. Soldiers are paid to die."

"Not uselessly."

"Maybe he will die anyway."

"Perhaps, but at least we will have tried to help him," the lieutenant said, exasperated by the captain.

"What is his life worth, anyway?"

"Captain, damn it, the man is a German soldier."

"And we are other German soldiers, and we have a duty to carry out our mission!"

"We will carry it out," the lieutenant said, bridling his anger. "There are two more soldiers. There is you and myself, and there is the French gendarme. Five of us. Five healthy men to capture an old man and his family."

The captain thought for a moment and then said, "I suppose you are right. Five of us should be enough. All right. One of your men stays with the wounded man."

He stood up. "But the rest of us go on." The lieutenant shrugged.

16

Another day was passing.

The snow lessened, and a glaring sun came through a break in the storm clouds. The sky, high above the world of the men on the mountain, seemed a gentle world.

By midday the temperature had soared, and the Basque and the others puffed and sweated as they climbed higher and deeper into the range. The glare of the sun almost blinded them, a glare made worse by the top crust, which turned to ice later in the day as the power of the sun waned. The glare became more of a hazard as the footing became more slippery.

They labored to a point near the top of a steep ridge. They had been more than two hours on the ridge.

The shepherd stopped and touched Perea's arm. Perea looked back and saw the small figures of men moving along the hill. They were a good distance away, but even at a distance one could see that the figures moved quickly, expertly.

"What do we do?" Perea asked.

The Basque said nothing but turned and indicated the others should follow. They made their way over the top of the ridge and down along the side of an imposing mountain. The Basque hurried now, glancing to the forest at his left, looking for something. After about fifteen minutes he turned and went into the forest. The others followed. There was a path that was almost unseen, but the sure feet of the Basque never wavered.

As the trees thinned at the base of the rock wall, the Basque found what he was looking for. A narrow defile that led through the mountain. They passed through the opening, the rock towering far above their heads until the defile began to widen and they emerged into a small, picturesque valley. The floor of the valley was flat and for the most part treeless. Without the carpet of snow it would have been pastureland.

The Basque stopped and sat down on the stump of a tree that had been felled by lightning. The others gazed about in wonder.

Isaac Bergman came over and sat down next to the shepherd. "What is this place?"

"When there are times of trouble, my people hide the sheep. It is a place known to few men."

Bergman nodded. "And the Germans?"

"They will go around the mountain. We will be many hours ahead after we cross the valley and climb over that far ridge."

Bergman looked across the valley and saw the steep walls. "Is there a pass?"

After a long silence the Basque answered. "No. We must climb."

A look of determination came over Bergman's face. "We will do it."

They sat in silence for a few moments. The Basque realized the other man was thinking about his wife, resting quietly in her mantle of white. He reached out and touched the other's arm. "I understand," he said.

Bergman looked into the shepherd's eyes and finally said, "Can you?"

The Basque looked down at the ground. "Yes. My wife was the whole world to me. And then one day there was an accident, and my whole world lay dead in the street." He paused and added, "We both have great cause to hate other men."

Bergman looked at the shepherd with compassion. A bond had grown between them. They were both men with the burdens of men.

"We must go," the Basque said, standing up, interrupting the reverie of Leah and Samuel, who were looking around with wonder at the peaceful valley.

The French guide led the Germans past the place where the Basque had taken the others into the forest. He did not give the seemingly impenetrable woods a second glance.

They went the long way around the mountain, and the captain was becoming annoyed because they could find no sign of the fugitives. When they came to the top of the ridge, Von Berkow stopped and scanned the horizon with his binoculars. He saw nothing.

"Where are they?" he asked the guide. "They must have gone another way."

"There is no other way," the guide said, and then

added, pointing back, "unless you think they climbed over those mountains."

Von Berkow looked at him with scorn. He pulled a map out of his pocket and held it so the guide could see it.

"This is where they are going?" von Berkow asked, pointing at the map. The guide nodded. "And this is where we are?"

The guide nodded again.

Von Berkow thought for a moment and then said, "They must be heading for this spot." He looked up at the fading light of the day. "We will travel all night again if we must."

The guide protested. "We must stop and rest. Everyone is tired. I don't know if I can keep going."

"You will keep going because if you do not," the captain said with a smile, "I will break your leg and leave you for the wolves."

Without a word the guide stood up, slung his rifle over his shoulder, and started back on the trail.

The Basque looked down the steep slope of the mountain. They had crossed the valley, climbed the high ridge, and now stood on the crest, bathed in the feeble moonlight, shivering in the freezing cold. It had been a four-hour climb to the top.

Once there was almost a disaster.

The Basque had been the first to climb over an overhanging ledge. There was no way to go around the ledge because the walls on each side were almost vertical. Leah came next, the shepherd reaching down to help pull her up.

Samuel followed. His hand was inches from the Basque when his foot gave way, his grip torn loose from the rock. Leah screamed as she watched her brother fall backward. Bergman looked up as his daughter screamed and saw the boy toppling backward. With a swiftness that was surprising, he jumped into the path of the falling boy. Samuel slammed into his father, and the momentum carried them both back, but Bergman had slowed the boy enough so when the two of them slid back, the force was broken, and Perea was able to stop them.

The boy looked around and thought his saviour had been Perea. He thanked him. He said nothing to his father.

The Basque and Leah watched as the men below rested for a few moments to catch their breath.

"That was close," the girl said.

The Basque looked at the girl. "Were you scared?"

"Yes."

"You become afraid for your family, but you are not afraid for yourself."

The girl said nothing, and the Basque grunted in admiration. He looked at her for a few moments. She realized he was staring at her and finally said, "Do you find me attractive?"

He nodded. "Yes."

They said no more, and soon the others were ready to come over the ledge.

They made it to the top without further incident.

The Basque stood at the crest thinking about the situation.

Leah came up and stood by the Basque's side. She rubbed her arms to warm them, but it did no good because the wind bit deep to the bone. The Basque unslung the *chahakoa* from his shoulder and sent a stream of wine into his mouth. When he finished, he passed the wineskin to the girl. She took it without hesitation and poured the wine into her mouth as expertly as the shepherd.

Samuel stood to the side, looking in awe at his sister. This was not the same girl who inspected glasses and silverware before she would use them. He shook his head, not quite sure if he approved the change in his sister.

The girl looked down the slope. It was treeless, the ice glistening in the moonlight. It looked like a great distance to the bottom.

"We must climb down?" she asked.

"No," the Basque said. "It would take too long. We would freeze before we got to the bottom."

"Then how?"

"We slide."

She looked at him without understanding.

"We make a toboggan," the Basque said.

He arranged them at the edge of the slope. Perea was in front, followed by Samuel, Bergman, and Leah. When they were locked together, their legs stretched alongside the person in front, the Basque took up the last position and began to shove them over the edge. "Hold on for your lives," he said, and then jumped down and locked his arms about the girl.

Almost immediately they picked up speed and hurtled down the icy slope. The wind tore at them and made it difficult to breathe. In twenty seconds they had come as far down the one side of the mountains as it had taken them half a day to climb up on the other. The boy's eyes were closed. He could not bear to look. The Basque buried his face in the girl's soft hair.

The human toboggan began to slow down as it plowed its way through the softer, heavier snow toward the bottom. And then the curve of the land grew more gentle. Finally, in a great spume of flying white powder, the toboggan slowed and came to a stop. No one moved for a few seconds, and then Perea spoke in a voice that was barely above a whisper. "We made it."

The people unloosened their grips, and the toboggan broke up into separate human beings. They looked at one another with disbelief on their faces. They had made it! They had been on the verge of death, in danger of being smashed to bits if they had crashed into a large boulder, but that hadn't happened. They had made it to the bottom.

The Basque was looking around for a place to spend the night. He inspected an outcropping of heavy rocks near the base of the mountain and finally found a small cave.

The Basque approached it warily, his rifle in his hands. He stepped inside and was gone for about a minute. He emerged and waved the others toward him.

"This is a good place to spend the night," he said.

Perea looked at him. "You want to stop?"

"Yes."

"And the Germans?"

"They are far behind us."

They moved into the cave. It was small, about twelve feet deep, ten feet wide, and about four feet high. They were forced to stoop or go about on their hands and knees. They gathered what brush and twigs they could find and built a windbreak at the front. They did not build a fire. A fire would be seen for many miles, and they dared not take the chance.

"Do animals live in this cave?" Samuel asked the Basque.

"Maybe before, but not now. There are no signs."

"What were they, the ones who lived here before, bears?"

"Perhaps. More likely wolves. This is too small and

too open for bears. They like to go as deep into the ground as they can for the winter."

"Yes, they hibernate," Isaac Bergman said. "An amazing process," he continued. "Hibernating animals fall into a deep sleep, and their body temperature lowers itself to the approximate temperature of the lair. The animal's metabolism slows down, and he uses very little energy. He can last four or five months that way without any ill effects."

"But if one showed up here, how would you kill him?" the boy asked his father. There was a trace of scorn in his voice.

Bergman looked at the boy and then away.

The Basque ate some bread.

When he was finished, he moved to the wall of the cave and rested his back. "It is time to sleep. We must go at daybreak." He pulled his cap over his eyes. Sleep came instantly.

The girl and Perea were already asleep. Only Bergman and his son remained awake.

A wolf howled in the distance.

Isaac Bergman rubbed his hands together and moved next to his son. The son looked at him for a moment and then gazed out through the little opening in front of the cave.

"The wolves are hunting."

"Yes," the boy said.

"And we are being hunted by animals who are worse than wolves."

Silence.

"What is wrong, my son?"

Silence.

"Is it that you find me useless here in the mountains? That I am weak when I should be strong? Is this what is bothering you?"

The boy said nothing. His head hung down.

"You are right to blame me for all of these things. I accept your scorn."

"What good does that do?"

"I taught you to respect the mind. I was wrong not to include the physical part of life in your instruction. I am sorry. But I am not sorry I taught you the strength of the mind. You should not despise me for that."

"I don't despise you," the boy said miserably. "It's just that I . . . we . . ."

"The power of the mind is a strong force, a more subtle force than a bullet or a knife, but it is every bit as powerful nonetheless."

Samuel said nothing.

"Why do you think we are here in this cave?" Bergman asked after a pause in the conversation.

The boy was puzzled. "What do you mean?"

"It is because of me, because of my power. I did not shoot at the Germans. I did not blow up their trains. No, I wrote about them. I told the truth as I saw it and exposed them for what they are. My words have wounded them as much as if I had shot them with a gun."

The boy's hostility was lessened.

"You admire this Basque shepherd a great deal, don't you?"

"He is a brave man. A very strong man. Where would we be if he was not with us?"

"We would be dead."

The bluntness of the words startled the boy. "You agree that you could not take his place?"

"Of course I couldn't, any more than he could take my place at the university. In a situation like this we need a man like him. But a man like him needs men like me, writers and thinkers who can cry out at injustice, who know right from wrong, who can help establish a world where a man like him is left in peace."

"I guess you are right."

"It is a fine thing to be strong and brave, but if you are an educated man, you must also understand that it is just as important to be mentally strong and brave."

The boy regarded his father. Some of the old admiration was coming back.

"Sometimes pure physical strength and pride in that strength can be merely stupidity masquerading as bravery," Bergman said. "A good example happened right here in these mountains."

"What happened?" the boy asked, curious now, again falling into the role of a student at the feet of his teacher. It was almost as if they had been transported in time and space and were back once again in the house in Paris.

"You've read the *Chanson de Roland?*"

The boy nodded.

"Pure myth. As the story is told, Roland is a brave hero who holds off the infidel and defends the pass until Charlemagne arrives. Too late to save Roland, of course, but the lad fought long and bravely enough to hold the pass until his uncle came back. Isn't that the way they tell the story?"

"Yes."

Bergman chuckled. "Roland's real name was Count Hroudland of Brittany, and he was a nephew of Charles, that much of the story is true. The rest of it is a fairy tale. What really happened was that Charles was retreating back to France from northern Spain. He had gone there to save the Christians from the Moors, but it seems the local Christians got along very well with the Moors and wanted no part of Charles and his Franks.

"Count Hroudland's forces fell far behind the main body as they went through the pass at Roncesvalles.

They were set upon by a band of men. Hroudland was too proud to sound the alarm. After all, wasn't he the nephew of Charles? What force could defeat him?

"So his heavily encumbered knights and soldiers in their metal armor fought and were slaughtered by their more mobile attackers. Oh, Hroudland blew the horn eventually, but it was too late. By the time Charles arrived, there wasn't a living soul on the scene. All the Franks were dead, and the attackers had melted into the mountains."

"That isn't the way they tell the story at school," the boy said.

"Another thing they didn't tell you was who the attackers were."

"The Moors? Wasn't it the Moors?"

Bergman chuckled again. "No, it was a band of the local Basque people."

"Basques?"

"Uh-huh. Our Basque shepherd is probably one of their descendants."

"Wow!" the boy said, all boy again, all pupil before the teaching of the master. "They can really tell you some lies in school, can't they?"

The man became very serious. "In Germany they are teaching young men of your age that Jews are scum, filthy creatures to be kicked and beaten, *animals* to be worked until they fall and die. This is what I was fighting against, and I fought with the weapons I know best, my brain and my pen. So don't be too angry with your father if he cannot climb mountains very well, or if he does not have strong arms. We must fight the enemy with our best weapons; each of us."

"I'm sorry," Samuel said. "I should not have been so stupid. But, Papa, I still want to be strong like the shepherd and . . . strong like you, too."

"I think you will. Yes, I think you will do that." He leaned over and kissed the boy on the cheek, and the boy did not pull away. "Now lie down and go to sleep. To-morrow we have another ridge to climb, and then we will be on the other side and in Spain. Can you believe it, my son. We will be in Spain."

The boy nodded and snuggled against the rough wall of the cave. He was asleep in ten seconds.

Now, Isaac Bergman thought, take some of your own advice and go to sleep yourself. You need it more than the boy, you old weakling.

But sleep did not come easily.

He thought of his wife. Who would have thought it possible that she could have been so aware of what was happening? So much aware that she took her own life to save ours? His Meriam? Take her life in that way? Not possible.

But it had happened.

He was sad. How he had taken her for granted. How he had forgotten the bright, inquisitive girl he had married and how, instead, he had come to think of her as another fixture in the house. What was it she had asked him? It hurt to think about it because she had said it only a little while before she . . . only a little while before. Do you think I am a good person? she had asked. A person? Dear Meriam, I'm sorry I was so busy thinking of you as a wife and a mother and a housekeeper I forgot you were also a person. But now I know it, and I will remember it and remember it and remember it until the last day of my life.

He stretched out, and he felt the ache in his muscles. They hurt, but it was not as bad as the night before. He had been sore this morning, but the constant walking and climbing had limbered him up, had drained all the soreness from him. The muscles would harden again in the night, but the climbing he would do in the morning would again soften them and work out the soreness.

Breathing had become more difficult as they climbed higher and higher. It was more of an effort to take ten steps than it had been at lower altitudes. It required more strength to fill one's lungs. The thinner air affected everything, even the trees. He had noticed they had become smaller the higher they grew on the mountains. The beech trees had disappeared entirely. Even for the trees it is more of a struggle to stay alive up here, he thought.

For the first time since he had escaped from Paris he had hope. They might live. A simple sentence, nothing complicated, but until now it was something he had not dared to hope. *They might live.* Most of the time he had not believed it would happen.

Memoirs of the condemned. The nightmarish escape from Paris. Living in cellars and attics. Listening to the rats at night. The bugs crawling over his body as he tried to sleep, the whimpering sleeplessness of his children, the soft crying of his wife. The fear that lived with them like another person, breathing with them, staying with them every minute of the day and night.

No, he had not thought any of them would live. Even when the Underground took him to Toulouse, and the shepherd came, and they were on the train. No, it never seemed possible. There was always something happening to remind him of his fear. The train wreck. The hostile Basque. The SS man in St. Limoux who had grabbed his hand.

The face of death. He had forgotten. He had been so exhausted and so occupied with climbing and keeping up with the Basque he had forgotten about that face. The face of the Devil. The eyes. The terrible eyes. And the hand. The claw of the Devil.

I wish I were a bear or some other animal with the ability to hibernate, he thought. It would be nice. We could barricade the door of this cave and go to sleep, and months would pass, and the Germans would have forgotten about us. We would wake up, and it would be spring on the mountain. A balmy day with the dew burning off and the flowers poking their heads through the warm earth. The sun would be shining, and we would all laugh and make our way down the other side of the mountain and find ourselves in Spain.

If only it were possible. And why shouldn't it be? Man is the highest order of mammal. Why is it that a bear, whose brain is nothing compared to man's, has the ability to control his body temperature, while man cannot? It shouldn't be difficult to research the subject. Maybe he would look into this phenomenon when he was safe and established at some university. . . .

What university? Where in Europe could he go? The Nazi plague was spreading everywhere. Soon all of Europe would be dominated by the swastika and the staccato beat of hobnail boots along the streets. Soon all of Europe would live in fear of the pounding on the door in the middle of the night. Where in Europe could he even *live*, much less be granted a post of importance at a university?

Which brought him to another interesting question. How was he going to live after these Underground people took him to wherever they had in mind? What work was he going to do? The Nazis had taken everything. And where *was* he going; where was the final destination? It couldn't be Spain. Not with Franco running the country. He wasn't a Nazi, nor was he a stooge of Hitler, but he was certainly friendly with the Germans. Maybe the Underground planned for him to go to Portugal. He would be safe there. Yes, safe, he thought, but for how long? A year? Two years?

America? England? Yes, he would probably have to go to America or England if he wanted to teach at a university again. And he did want to teach again. He wanted to do a paper about the philosophy of terorrism. It was an interesting subject.

Go to sleep, you old fool, he told himself. Here you are, half frozen on the side of a mountain, wolves howling in the night, being chased by the Germans, and you lie here thinking about the next textbook you are planning to write.

17

The two old gravediggers shuffled to the side of the open pit. They were very old men with lined faces and skin the color of a foggy day at sea. Their clothes were tattered. Stained, grimy caps shielded their heads from the fine but insistent rain. Their shoes were encased in clumps of mud. They carried shovels on their shoulders.

There were five bodies beside the pit. Each was wrapped in cheap, heavy cloth.

"Five," one gravedigger said.

"That makes forty this week."

"I am getting too old for so many."

"The Germans do not seem to care."

The man looked at the bodies. "Five more nameless paupers; that's all we ever get in this place."

"We are all paupers. I have been digging graves here in Toulouse for sixty years. You would think I have earned a rest. But no, I have never saved any money, so I must work."

They stood beside the open pit, which others had dug earlier in the day. To the right of the pit stood a row of freshly filled mounds of earth.

"At this rate there will soon be no more room."

"Then we will be out of jobs."

"Then we might as well dig our own pit."

A German army truck drove up. Two men in SS uniforms climbed out of the cab and went to the back of the truck. They dragged out another cloth-covered corpse. They carried it to the side of the pit and dropped it on the ground next to the other bodies.

"Another one come for your blessing, old man," the driver said. "From the prison."

"What did this one do?"

"Who knows?"

"You kill them, and you don't know what for?"

"Another prisoner, another scoundrel."

"French or German?" the old gravedigger asked.

"Don't be smart."

"Should we go through his pockets, or have you saved us the trouble?" the other gravedigger asked.

The SS man sneered. "Go ahead, use your mouth. Soon it will be full of flies, and you will be the one who lies there and hears the rain of dirt coming down on your head."

"It happens to all of us. Even SS men."

"Good thing you are so old, or I would be tempted to teach you some respect," the German said angrily.

The other gravedigger went nearer to the new corpse. "This one smells to high heaven," he said. He sniffed and wiped his nose with his hand.

The German laughed. "This one should smell. He was in a closet for a few days. Just lying there."

"Why a closet?"

The German shrugged. "No reason. They just forgot he was there. Somebody finally smelled him. He should be ripe enough for you now."

The gravedigger spat on the ground. "You have no respect for the dead."

The Germans got back in their truck and drove away.

"Should we see if this one has anything worth taking?"

The older gravedigger shook his head. "The ones from the prison never have anything."

"You can never tell."

"You are wasting your time," the older gravedigger said as he watched the other one begin to open the sack.

He pulled the strings apart and drew back the cloth. "Mother of God!" the gravedigger said, stepping back from the exposed corpse. "Look at the face on this one!"

The older gravedigger went over and grimaced when he saw what had been hidden by the dirty cloth. It was the face of a man who had died in agony. The mouth was open, exposing the raw gums where teeth had been pulled or torn away. The eyes were open. The veins in the whites had popped. Dried blood was caked around the nose and ears. The hair was singed as if it had been burned by fire. The body was smeared with excrement.

"Smell the shit," the older gravedigger said.

"It is more than shit."

"The body is causing the smell."

"This one did not die in bed."

"This one prayed for death."

Two men walked up as the gravediggers stared at the tortured face of the dead man. They stopped when they saw the face of the exposed body. They were tough-looking men. One was slender but looked strong and wiry. He wore a short coat that was not long enough for his arms. His wrists were bony. The other man was shorter but stockier and with the arms of a much larger man. He wore a beret and smoked a cigarette, which he never took out of his mouth.

"What are you doing with that body?" the slender one asked. His voice was flat and hard.

"What are we doing?" the older gravedigger said. "Why we are preparing to enter it in a beauty contest."

The stocky man blew smoke from his mouth. The slender one looked at him with disgust. "How much do you want for that body?"

"You want to buy this body?"

"I have come here for that body. I mean to have it."

"But it is only the body of a scoundrel from the prison."

"How much?"

The old gravedigger's face contorted as he chewed his almost toothless gums. He was thinking, trying to understand what there was about this corpse that would make someone want it.

"This man was French?" he asked.

"Yes."

"And the Germans did this to him?"

"Yes."

"And you are French? From Toulouse?"

"I am French. From Paris," the slender one said. "He is from Toulouse," he said, indicating the stocky man.

The old gravedigger understood.

"Take the body."

"How much?"

"He is a hero. I do not charge for heroes."

"Thank you."

The two strangers covered the body with the cloth. The stocky one picked up the bundle and placed it on his shoulder. He treated the weight as if it were a feather.

"What was his name?" the old gravedigger asked the slender one.

"Renoudot."

"You knew him?"

"Yes."

"Underground?"

"Yes."

"If I were only younger," the old gravedigger sighed. "Ahhh, if I were only younger."

The slender man smiled for the first time. "You are doing your part, Grandfather."

The old gravedigger pointed at the body. "You want to bury him somewhere else?"

"In a grave of honor."

"That is good. This pauper's grave is no place for a hero to spend eternity."

"He will be with friends."

"Rest in peace, Renoudot," the old gravedigger said softly. "France thanks you."

The two men left with the corpse. The gravediggers watched until they were gone. They leaned on their shovels in a pose they had come to assume without thinking about it.

"They were willing to pay for that body," the other gravedigger complained.

"I would not take their money," the old man said

"You are getting soft."

"Let's get to work," the older gravedigger said, pushing a cloth-covered body into the pit. It hit the bottom with a crunch. When the five bodies filled the bottom, the two old gravediggers began to shovel in the muddy dirt. Water dripped from their caps and the tips of their noses.

"I hate working in the rain," the old gravedigger said. "It takes more dirt to fill up the hole."

18

There was silence in the mountains. A time of peace in the world. The black of night was dissolving into the murky gray that precedes the first light.

Samuel stepped out of the cave and gazed about. Nothing moved. It was a world of the dead. Not a bird or an animal moved. There was no wind. It was a world where a whisper would break the silence like a thunderclap.

The Basque was the next to awaken. The others followed within minutes. No one talked. They munched on their meager rations and drank wine from the *chabakoa*.

As soon as there was enough light to see without chancing a broken leg, Perea shouldered his pack. The supplies had dwindled, and there was need for only the one small pack. The Basque left his pack in the cave. He slung his rifle across his back and stepped outside to look for the easiest way over the next ridge. The elder Bergman stretched his muscles. He had done better without his pack, the boy thought. He doesn't have the strength of the other men, and he shouldn't pretend he has. There is no shame in that.

They began to climb toward the crest. It went slowly. Samuel knew that neither his father nor his sister nor he himself had the strength of two days ago. Their bodies were wearing down. But they were doing their best, and it seemed good enough for the shepherd. He had said nothing about moving faster during the previous day. It was obvious that he himself could have gone faster, but he remained with the others.

The boy found himself next to the Basque as the group climbed over a rocky abutment and made its way up the face of the snowy slope.

They climbed side by side in silence for several minutes, the boy taking great pains to move in a natural manner, hiding the awkward motion of his lame leg as much as possible. If the Basque noticed what the boy was doing, he said nothing.

The boy wanted to talk.

"My sister said she tried to get you to teach her to speak Basque."

The man shook his head. "It is too difficult."

"I've read about Basque in books," the boy said, grateful that the Basque seemed willing to talk. "They say it is unlike any other language spoken in Europe."

"That is true."

"Do you know why?"

"There are many stories."

"Do you know them?"

The Basque nodded. "There is an old legend that says we are descended from Tubal, the fifth son of Japheth, who was the son of Noah. Tubal came here before the

Tower of Babel was built, so he alone spoke the pure language of the Garden of Eden."

The boy was listening intently.

The Basque looked at him and said, "So when you are listening to us talk among ourselves, you are listening to the language in which Adam wooed Eve."

The boy's eyes widened. "Do you believe that?"

"Why not believe it?"

"But it's such a . . . such a fairy tale," the boy sputtered. "Can you prove it is true?"

"Is there anyone who can prove that it is not?"

"If it is true, it means your people have been in these mountains since the days of Noah."

"We have been here a long time. The same people. Speaking the same language. Raising cattle and sheep and families. We have been happy. We fish, and we hunt, and we live in the mountains."

"Do you like to hunt?"

"Sometimes," the Basque said. "I hunt deer."

"And bear? Do you hunt bears?"

The Basque smiled. "There are not many bears left. Even if there were many, I would not hunt bears. They are too dangerous. If you wound one and don't kill it, there is a good chance it will kill you. But there is another reason, too. I think deer meat is sweeter than bear meat."

"But you have killed bears?"

"Yes, I have killed bears."

"And wolves?"

"I have killed many wolves," the Basque said. His voice was grim. "They are the enemies of my sheep and myself. However, I have friends who help me with the wolves."

"Friends?"

"Yes, friends. They are with the sheep right now."

Or at least he thought they were. His *Komondorok* were either tending the sheep, or they were dead. He had no doubts about his dogs. The thought of his sheep bothered him. He had been away a long time, too long, and many things could have happened. The *Komondorok* would protect the sheep from wolves, but could they protect them from everything else? Perhaps men who came with guns to steal the sheep.

Without realizing it, he began to climb faster. The boy struggled to keep pace with him.

"What is your favorite hunting?" he asked.

"Wild pigeons," the Basque answered. "I have not done it for years. The way the *Euscaldanac* hunt pigeons is more like a big party than a hunt. We build a high platform in the tallest tree. It is called the Tower of Death, and a man waits there. On the ground are tall nets of a very fine mesh, almost as fine as the web of a spider. The birds appear, swooping down the ravine in formation, following their leaders. The man in the Tower of Death throws whittled discs which fly through the air in the manner of a hawk. The terrified birds swoop down to get away from the hawks, and they fly into the nets, and their wings are caught in the netting. A top net is lowered to trap them, and the men come. They pluck the birds from the nets the way other men pluck grapes from the vines. It is a *harvest* of birds."

The boy was surprised. It didn't sound much like a sport, more like a slaughter.

"We would take the pigeons to the village and have a big feast. Wine would flow, and there would be music and dancing, and nobody had a care in the world."

"Do you do this often?" the boy asked.

"Years ago, but no more."

"Why not?"

"It is the men from the village who do this."

The boy shook his head. "I don't understand."

"I am no longer part of the village," the Basque said, and he continued to climb.

The boy slowed down because his leg began to hurt. The Basque did not take notice and moved ahead.

What would become of his family? Where would they live? He suddenly realized he didn't care what the others in his family did; he cared only about what he would do. He wanted to stay with the Basque and become a man of strength. He wasn't sure he wanted to do it for the rest of his life, but right now it was what he wanted to do. That was what was important. To do what you wanted to do now. I have lived fifteen years, and I have been going to school and wearing nice clothes and eating the right foods and getting enough sleep at night, and all of these things I have done because someone else wanted me to do them. It is time I started living for now instead of preparing for a future that might never happen.

I could be dead right now.

I have come near death many times in the past few months, and what if I had died? What would my life, every single day of my life, every single hour and minute, what would it all have meant if I had never done one single thing I wanted to do? Not to do it for someone else but to do it for myself and to know I have done it for myself. I have lived my life as if it were to go on forever. I was buying my future with my present, and how cheated I will be if it turns out there is no future, only the past, and this past, which I squandered, was all I had, and there would be no more.

Consider all the things you have never done. You have never gone away by yourself. You have always been "the son" as you traveled with your family. You have never smoked a cigarette or a cigar or a pipe. You have never fired a rifle or a pistol. You have never—and this was a subject he was only beginning to learn about, furtively, in whispers with friends from school, sniggering, trying to appear nonchalant and failing in the attempt, looking at the pictures one of the boys had bought on the street and was having a devil of a time concealing in the pages of his schoolbooks—yes, you have never made love to a woman. What would it be like, he wondered. To be in bed with a naked girl. A girl like Rachel, who had lived in the house next door in Paris. Rachel was the same age, but she looked more like a woman than he like a man. That was because of her . . . breasts. God, were they big. As big as a full-grown woman's. *What would it be like if you were in bed and those big breasts were pushed up against your chest, the chest that was beginning to sprout hairs?* How proud he was of those hairs. He felt like a man every time he stood naked to the waist in front of a mirror. At first he had tried to count them one by one. Now they were beyond counting, and isn't it a sign that you are a man, no longer a boy, when the hairs on your chest multiplied beyond counting?

He waited for his sister.

"Are you tired?" she asked when she climbed to his side.

"No."

"Why did you stop?"

"I thought I would wait for you."

"That is very nice."

"How do you feel?" he asked. "Are your legs sore?"

"When I first wake up. But after I walk and climb for a time, the soreness is gone."

"That's because the muscles loosen up."

"We're almost to the top," she said.

The boy looked up and saw the Basque was already at

the crest. "A few minutes," he said, and began climbing again.

The last to arrive at the top were Bergman and Perea. They looked over the other side and saw the slope fall away toward a thickly forested ravine. It would be a much faster climb down than it had been up. Not only was it downhill, but also the floor of the ravine was much higher up the slope on the Spanish side than on the French.

The Basque pointed out their route. "We will follow the ravine around that hill. There is a gorge with a stream that runs through the ravine. We will follow the stream for about a mile. There is a ford we will cross and then a pass that leads out of the mountains into the foothills."

"Won't the stream be frozen?" the boy asked.

"No. It will freeze soon, but now it will be running. And because this sun is causing much melting, it will be running fast."

"It is rugged country," Perea said.

"Yes," the Basque said. "At least we go downhill from now on."

"Thank God," Bergman said. "I don't think I ever want to climb another hill in my life."

The Basque studied the ground. "We will go down the slope in that direction," he said, pointing slightly to the right. "I don't want to end up directly below us. There are deep pockets of snow down there."

"How do you know?" the boy asked.

The Basque pointed to the bottom of the hill. "Do you see those big piles of snow down there, the ones standing higher than the snow around them?"

"The mound? Yes, I see them," the boy said.

"Those are big piles of rocks that have been carried

down the face of the mountain by ice. The ice scooped out a great chunk of the earth and carried it down the face, breaking it up into smaller pieces as it went along. This happened many years ago, thousands of years ago, but the big scoop is still there, and it is filled with snow. The snow is soft. It would be difficult to cross. So we will not cross it but go down alongside."

The boy nodded. He was learning about mountains.

CRAAAAAAAAAAACK!!!!

The sound of a high-powered rifle. The reverberations echoed and re-echoed up and down the canyon, bouncing back and forth off the faces of the mountains.

CRAAAAAAAAAAACK!!!!

The bouncing echoes made each shot sound like a hundred.

"Look," Perea said. There was horror in his voice.

They looked in the direction he was pointing and saw the dark moving specks coming down the ravine to the base of the face they had just climbed. They counted the specks. Four. Moving rapidly.

They did not see the fifth one dressed in white.

There was no doubt in anyone's mind about the nature of the specks.

19

Perea dropped down on the snow and peered over the edge of the ridge at the advancing men. They had reached the base of the hill and were beginning to climb. They were moving rapidly, and he guessed they would reach the crest in less than two hours.

The Basque started down the other side. "We must reach the ravine before the Germans get to the top. There is cover in the trees. They will not be able to shoot at us."

They started down the slope, moving recklessly, with little grace, not worrying about each rock and ledge because they were fleeing for their lives. There could be no more optimistic dreams, no more fanciful hopes. The enemy had seen them and shot at them.

Isaac Bergman slipped and skidded about thirty feet, his fall checked by a snowbank. He was unhurt and, spurred by the goad of terror, twisted his body sideways and was again moving downhill in seconds.

They reached the bottom of the slope and the first trees in less than an hour. They stopped, panting for breath, sweat glistening on their faces, their hearts pounding. The sun was up, and already the day was warm. Later it would get blisteringly hot in the glare on the open face of the snow, but they would be protected by the trees in the ravine.

They rested for five minutes.

Perea sat on a rock, thinking. They had come so far and so close to victory it seemed unfair to lose now. His mission had been to save Isaac Bergman, and he had done it. Almost. Where was justice if his victory were snatched away from him now?

"I am staying here," he said.

The others looked at him without understanding.

"But the Germans," Bergman said. "They will be here soon. You can't stay here."

"I am staying here *because* the Germans will be here soon," Perea said quietly.

"What do you mean?"

"The Germans will reach the crest. They will see our footsteps and follow them down. They will pass the trees at this very spot." He patted his rifle. "I will be here waiting for them."

"That is suicide!" Bergman said.

"I will delay them. It will give you more time to escape."

The Basque was silent for a moment. He looked strangely at Perea and said, "Why do you do this?"

"Why? Why? Because I am mad, you are mad, the world is mad! What difference does it make? Go, damn it. I will stay here and stop the Germans."

"We cannot leave you," Isaac Bergman said.

Perea became angry. "What is this? Who the hell are you to make such a choice? You must go. Why do you think the Underground went to all this trouble? Why has Renoudot died? Bergman, you have no choice. The Nazis want to capture you, and we do not want them to capture you. Now get the hell out of here!"

He turned to the Basque. "I will kill as many Germans as I can. Good luck."

"You are willing to die for this man?" the Basque asked.

"Yes."

The Basque turned and without a word started down the ravine toward the gorge that followed the path of the stream. The boy followed, and the girl, after looking once more at Perea, walked away quickly. Bergman stood for a few seconds, his eyes on Perea, his lower lip trembling. He wanted to say something, but he could not think of any words. What is there to say to a man who is going to die for you?

"Please go," Perea said. "I must find a good place to fight the Germans. The longer you stay here, the more you endanger my life."

Bergman touched the man on the shoulder. He took a last look into the man's eyes and then went after the others. He did not look back.

Perea watched them go. He did not move for a full minute after Bergman disappeared into the trees.

They were gone. He was alone.

He walked along the fringe of the trees until he saw what he was looking for. A good-sized rock, about three feet high, set back about twenty feet in the trees. He moved behind the rock and placed his rifle on top of it. The Germans would be following the footsteps in the snow, and they would pass directly in front of him at a distance of thirty feet. The trees were sparse. They would not block his shot.

Leaving his rifle on the rock, he moved to the edge of the trees and looked up the slope. He saw nothing. The Germans were still climbing up the other side. He went back to the rock and took out one of his carefully hoarded cigarettes and lit it. He inhaled deeply and blew the smoke into the branches above.

In his heart he knew he had small hope of living. Yes, he might kill one of them, and with luck, two. But what about the other two? When the first shot rang out, the element of surprise would be gone, and the other three men would hurl themselves in the snow and roll over and return the rifle fire. And then there would be two or three guns against his one. And, he reminded himself, these are not children who are coming down the mountain. They are trained killers who will react instantly to the first shot. They will know what to do.

He looked back into the woods. The farther back he looked, the denser the trees became. I will fall back that way, he thought. They will come after me, but I will shoot at them and teach them to come slowly.

He felt sorry for himself. He was about to be killed, even as the activities of the Underground were really getting started. They were going to give the Germans one hell of a time. *And I am not going to be a part of it.* When he had involved himself with the Underground, he knew he might someday be called upon to die. But he hadn't known it would be so soon. Why did it have to happen now? Why couldn't it have waited a few years? By then he would have blown bridges and mined trains and thrown a few knives into a few German throats, gotten his share, so to speak, and by then he would not feel cheated when it came his turn to die.

"Thy will be done, Lord," he murmured, and made the sign of the cross. If it is my destiny to die now, so be it, he thought. But I will take a German or two with me, he promised himself, his mouth forming a grim smile.

He threw the cigarette butt to the ground and stomped his boot on it. He peered up.

There they were.

The dark silhouettes of men coming to the crest of the ridge. The sun was shining down at an angle that prevented him from seeing anything except the dark shape of each man against the sky. There were five of them. Five? Where had the other one come from? He had seen only four when they were at the base of the hill.

He watched them come down the slope, moving quickly, skidding, sliding, breaking the force of each slide with their feet. They move well, he thought. Much faster than we have been moving, he thought with a tinge of envy.

He went back to the rock and took up his position behind it. He checked his rifle, making sure there was a shell in the bore and the weapon ready to fire. There was nothing more he could do. He had two cigarettes in his pocket, and he wanted to smoke, but he dared not, afraid the telltale wisp of smoke might give him away. His one chance of success lay in complete surprise. The Germans would be looking at the footprints that continued down the ravine. They would not suspect that anyone was waiting at this place, or at least he hoped they would not suspect.

They were coming closer. In five minutes they would be at the base of the slope. They would be directly in his line of fire in seven or eight minutes.

He patted the stock of his weapon. Yes, there was one thing that could make them stop.

They were coming. Five of them. He realized why he

had only counted four when he was on the crest and they were a good distance away. The fifth was dressed in white. He had blended into the background of snow.

Perea settled his rifle on the rock. He began tracking the first man with the sight. Another *fifty* feet . . . it would soon start . . . *forty* . . . the surprise would be over . . . *thirty* . . . but there would be one less German to contaminate the world . . . *twenty* . . . the man was looking down at the footprints, not bothering with the trees . . . *ten* . . . he came abreast of Perea.

CRAAAAAACK!!!!

The bullet caught the man on the side of the head, just above the ear. It tore the back of his head off, splintering the bone, smashing through the soft tissue of the brain, splattering gouts of flesh, bone, blood, and brains into the snow. The man fell forward, dead before he knew he had been shot, not a man anymore, a corpse, a piece of matter returned to earth.

Perea shifted the barrel of his rifle and squeezed off a second shot at another German.

CRAAAAAAACK!!!!

The German had started to fling himself sideways at the sound of the first shot, and although only a second passed between the two shots, it was enough to keep him from getting killed. The bullet whirred into the top of his left thigh. The man screamed as he pitched forward into the snow. He grabbed at the leg, and the snow beneath and around began to turn red.

The other Germans had dropped and rolled on the ground. They began firing into the woods. Perea fired back at one of them, but the bullet whistled harmlessly over the man's head. A barrage of answering shots returned, and he ducked behind the rock. Now was the time to move. He crawled on all fours toward the denser clusters of trees, keeping the rock between himself and the Germans. He worked his way toward another large rock, crawled behind it and stopped. He listened, but he could hear no movement. It would take the Germans several minutes to get up enough courage to move forward. It would also take them time to realize that there was no one at the place where the first shots were fired from.

He was buying time.

A minute passed. More minutes. Finally he heard a body moving over the ground. He carefully peered over the rock. He could see nothing, but he heard the sound again. He pulled the trigger on his rifle, and the bullet screamed and then screamed again as it ricocheted off a boulder. He dropped behind the rock as a bullet whined over his head. Another rifle began firing from his right-front quarter.

They have spread out, he thought. He fired toward the unseen man on his right-front quarter and was rewarded by two fast shots from the rifle directly in front of him. The first bullet whistled over his head, but the second hit the rock and caromed off with an angry screech into the air, splintering the rock and spraying his face with little bits of grit. One landed right in his left eye.

Jesus! The pain!

He blinked his eye. He wanted to scream but held back the urge and bit down on his tongue. He blinked the eye several times, and it was torture. He held it open. The vision was blurred. He could make out only the shapes of objects, not details.

Wonderful, he thought. Now I must fight these bastards with only one eye. He closed the hurting eye and peered over the top of the rock with his good one. He detected movement and fired again. The bullet crashed into the ground not far in front of his protective rock. He had lost his depth perception.

There was a sound of movement by the man to his right-front quarter, and he fired his rifle in the general direction. The bullet passed harmlessly through the leaves of the trees. He no longer bothered to aim the rifle, simply pointed it. There was no longer any doubt about the outcome of this battle.

He suddenly thrust his rifle on top of the rock and fired directly in front of him. At least that will keep them wary. How are they to know I can see with only one eye? He squeezed the trigger again, and this time the bullet went in the direction of the man in his right-front quarter.

A thought occurred to him. *Where was the other one?*

There had been five. The first had died. He knew this because he had seen the man's brains blasted out of his head. The second man had been wounded. From the sounds the man made it must be a bad wound. Perea could still hear the muffled sobbing in the distance.

That left three more. The one in front of him. The one to his right-front quarter. And the other? He looked to his left. He could see nothing. He decided to fall back farther.

Using his one eye to see, he crawled around a tree and passed several clumps of rocks. The trees began to thin out again. What now? He heard a sound in front of him and realized it was the sound of running water. The stream! If he could make it to the stream, he might escape. While the Germans hunted for him, he could move down the stream on the other side. He could establish another post and wait for them. Hopefully he could pull another surprise attack. He smiled even though his eye felt like there was fire in it. He was not finished with these Germans. Not yet.

He crawled toward the sound of the water, carefully

looking over his shoulder every few seconds. He could detect no movement of pursuit.

The trees thinned away to nothing as he came closer to the edge of the stream, and the snow reappeared, first in patches, then in a continual white blanket that ended at the edge of the water.

He looked back into the woods. He watched for half a minute, immobile, watching for the slightest trace of movement. He could see nothing. He studied the stream. The best way to cross would be to dash across as quickly as possible. The stream was not very wide at this point, and there was a flat rock in the middle. He gauged the distance as best he might with his one good eye. It looked as if he could make it.

Now, he thought, jumping up and running to the stream. He came to the edge, leapt for the rock, and made it easily. Even as he landed on the rock, his good eye detected motion at the edge of the trees.

For the very smallest portion of a second he realized it was a man, and the man was aiming a rifle. In the microsecond between the time the bullet caught him directly in the chest and hurled him backward, already dead, into the freezing water, he saw his killer. It was the fifth man, the one dressed in white.

The man was the last thing on earth he saw because he was dead as his body splashed noisily into the freezing water.

He didn't even know it was cold.

20

Gunther von Berkow was livid with rage. The delay had cost them over half an hour. Bergman had gained time because of that damned sniper.

"Well?" he asked the Wehrmacht lieutenant, who was wrapping a bandage around the wounded soldier's leg. The man had lost considerable blood and was in great pain. The bullet had gone through the upper part of the leg near the groin, and it had cracked a bone, flicking off chips and burying them in the flesh. Every movement brought excruciating agony.

"We have no drugs for him," the lieutenant said. "And the other one," he said, indicating the French gendarme, half of whose head lay splattered in the snow, "forget him. He's dead."

"I know that," Gunther von Berkow said, trying to

remain patient with this idiot. "I meant that it is time for us to go."

"Go?"

"Yes, go! After Bergman."

"But we can't leave this man here alone," the lieutenant protested.

Von Berkow remained calm. "We are down to three men. The three of us must continue our mission."

"You intend to leave this wounded man here? Exposed to the sun?"

"We will move him under those trees. He will be protected."

"But he will die."

"If he is going to die, he will die if we are with him or if we are not."

"I cannot leave this man alone," the lieutenant said. He indicated the remaining soldier. "Stoecker will remain with him."

The captain's eyes narrowed. He smiled. "Stoecker is coming with us. We will need him. Enough of this talk. We are leaving right now."

The lieutenant wavered before the eyes that bored into him and through him. "You would leave a German soldier to die?" he asked in a voice that was more a whisper.

"No, not to die. We are going to finish what we set out to do. When we capture Bergman, we will come back here to take care of this wounded man. This good German soldier," he added sarcastically.

"What if he dies?"

"Then he dies."

"It would be a shame."

"More of a shame than to fail?"

"Success is that important?"

"Success is everything."

The lieutenant felt drained. This captain had defeated him. He consoled himself by thinking there was nothing he could do for the soldier at any rate. He had bandaged the wound. It was all he could do.

"Very well," he said, "let's go."

"I don't expect any more ambushes. We will move as swiftly as we can."

They moved off, von Berkow leading the way at a rapid walk, trotting at times when the ground was flat or sloped downward. The other two kept pace. He never paused. There was no need. The footprints in the snow made a clear road to follow. Their path moved at an angle, bringing them closer and closer to the stream. He is headed toward the stream, von Berkow thought; therefore, this Basque guide must know where there is a ford. Very well, we will let him lead us to the ford.

He smiled as he trotted along. It would not be long before he came to the end of his long chase. That it had been a difficult chase would make the ending more rewarding. The things we get with the most difficulty are the things we treasure most. He could not believe this Jew had given him so much trouble. A miserable Jew! *No, you are wrong. It isn't the Jew.* It was the others, the ones who were helping him. These Underground traitors. Swine! Pretending to be waiters. Pretending to be bakers. Pretending to be Gypsies. No wonder they were so difficult to catch; they were always pretending to be something else.

Never mind, their days were numbered. When the SS took full control of France, they would take care of these presumptuous dogs. The SS would make them humble themselves and grovel on their knees. The dogs would beg to be killed.

He could hardly wait.

He wanted to make all of these pigs beg and whine. He wanted them to kneel at his feet and lick his boots and ask for mercy in the form of a bullet in the brain. The SS would know how to deal with them. Those who could not learn to be good slaves were going to be dead slaves. But not before they learned the agony of hell on earth, not before they learned to hate their own bodies and to hate the mother who bore them into the world.

The soldier with the wounded leg watched them go. In a minute they had dropped below a sloping knoll and were lost to his view. He moved and grimaced as a chip of bone dug into his flesh. He looked at his leg. The bandage was beginning to turn red. He became aware of a hazy film in front of his eyes. He rubbed them with the back of a gloved hand. The pain of this movement caused him to stop. He opened his eyes. The hazy film was still there. What was the matter? he thought.

The blood began to seep from under the bandage. The wound hurt more than before. Why did that bastard of a lieutenant tie the bandage so tight? He reached for the knot, and although every movement sent pain shooting through his body, he managed, after a few fumbling attempts, to untie it. He unwrapped the bandage and exposed the wound.

Mother of God!

He stared. The back half of the leg was missing. One bullet did this? One bullet? Tore off half my leg? And am I to be a cripple for the rest of my life?

He looked in the direction the others had taken. Dirty, rotten bastards. Leaving me here alone. The solidarity of the German soldier—ha! That was a farce. And Stoecker is supposed to be my friend. Stoecker, who was always borrowing cigarettes and money. Some friend. I even found him a woman in St. Limoux, and now the louse goes off and leaves me here in the snow with half a leg. Some friend. Shit!

A pair of narrow eyes glared at him from the shadows beneath the trees. Another pair joined them. Soon there were six pairs.

The German soldier looked up when he heard a sound. It came from deeper in the trees. He strained to see through the hazy film before his eyes. A gray shape moved from one tree to another. What's that? he thought. Another sniper?

And then he saw the eyes. First one pair. Then another. And then a gray shape moving steadily forward.

He froze. Not a sniper, a wolf! Two wolves. There was more movement. How many wolves were there, he wondered.

His vision was becoming more blurred, his senses more dulled even as they were screaming danger signals.

"Come out and fight," he shouted in a hoarse voice, not knowing what he was shouting, afraid on the one hand and beyond fear on the other.

"Come out and fight, you cowards!

"Cowards! Bastards!"

He grasped his rifle. He tried to raise it and could not. The loss of blood had been too much. His strength was gone. He could see the wolves coming, and he could do nothing about it. His eyes began to close.

He heard an unearthly scream, and his eyes popped open. It was a silent scream heard only in his own mind as he felt the hot breath of the wolf's jaws as the animal stared at him from six inches away. It was the last of his consciousness.

His eyes closed, never to open again.

21

————————————————————————

The Basque had come to the gorge and was following the stream. It was running rapidly. The hot sun was melting the soft top snow before it could frost and turn to ice. After the next snowfall a heavier frost would form, the stream would begin to move more sluggishly, and ice would form along each bank, building up and moving closer toward one another, narrowing the stream until the process was complete, the stream iced over for the winter.

They followed the tortuous bends of the gorge. Finally the Basque saw the ford. About a hundred meters farther. It looked passable.

The Basque was thinking of Perea. Why had the man sacrificed his life? He was not even being paid, and he would do a thing like this. Was his passion for this *cause* so great that he was willing to sacrifice his life?

It could not only be love for this family, he thought. Perea did not know them even as well as I do, which is not well at all. Yet he is willing to die for them. The Basque shook his head.

He felt a strange emotion. He wanted to help Bergman escape because Perea had died for him. He did not want a brave man to die for nothing. And then again, there was the other one, the Frenchman Renoudot, whom he had disliked, but who also had been brave enough to die for his beliefs. Two men in their graves because they believed enough in their cause to die for it.

His mouth was dry. He wanted to drink some wine, or better, a bit of Izarra, a delicious liqueur. There was neither Izarra to drink nor time to drink it. The Germans could be upon them at any time. It depended on how long Perea was able to hold them.

Probably not for long. He is only one man, and they are many. So he will die.

The boy was plodding along, slipping, trotting, but keeping up with him. *This boy will not die. Nor the girl, nor the father.*

He surprised himself. Two brave men had died, and now the challenge was his, the two deaths becoming a symbol of his assumption of the role of saviour. And then there was the dead mother, sacrificing herself for the others. The boy and the girl he had grown to admire. They had heart. The boy, especially, because he had the bad leg. In all the time they had been together, in filthy Gypsy wagons, in snowstorms, climbing steep hills, in all this time and with all these obstacles he had never heard the boy complain. He sighed and shook his head. This was not what he had in mind when he agreed to smuggle four people through the mountains. He had not asked for this. But it had happened.

He accepted it.

They came to the ford, and the Basque realized it was deep, the running water churning and frothing. It was passable but dangerous.

"I will go first. Follow in my steps," he said, carefully finding his first footing. The water swirled about his boots, four inches up from the heel. He took another step, and his foot found a rock. He rose out of the water, his feet barely covered with two inches of water. Two more steps. One more and he was in water to his knees. Three more steps, and he was on another rock. The water was shallow from the rock to the bank. Five quick steps, and he was out of the water, safe on dry land on the other side.

"Hurry," he said, and the girl took her first step. She went to the first rock. She went into the deeper water and waded quickly to the last rock. She came safely to the far bank.

"Brrrrr, it's really cold," she said to the Basque.

Isaac Bergman took twice as long as his daughter, but he made the crossing without incident. He began stomping around, warming his feet, keeping the circulation going, and trying to prevent the water from freezing to ice.

It was Samuel's turn. A few steps and he was on the first rock. He smiled across the stream at the others. He stepped down from the rock and entered the deepest part of the stream. One step . . . two steps . . . and then it happened. It was the fault of his bad leg. He swung it forward, and it slipped on a smooth part of the stream's bottom. The leg went out from under him; with a yelp he fell down, and the force of the water began carrying him downstream.

Bergman shouted and started for the edge of the water as if to throw himself in. The Basque grabbed him. "Let me go. Can't you see my son is drowning?"

The Basque pushed him back. He went to the bank and held his *makhila* out over the water. The boy grabbed the end of the stick, and the Basque pulled him to the edge of the stream. With his free hand he reached out and grabbed the boy's coat, pulling him roughly forward where he landed with a "splat" on the dry ground.

The boy's face was blue, and he was gasping. The Basque pulled him to his feet.

And then they heard the sound of rifle fire. First one shot. Then another. Then many shots.

They all had the same thought. Perea.

"You must keep moving," the Basque said to the boy. He turned to the other two. "We must all keep moving. If we don't, we will freeze, or the Germans will come and shoot us."

"Aren't we in Spain?" the girl asked.

"Yes."

"How can the Germans follow us now?"

"They respect no law," Bergman said.

"We must keep moving," the Basque said.

"Yes," Bergman said, grabbing his son's arm and pushing him down the gorge.

The Basque looked back up the gorge. He could not see any pursuit. He looked up through a cleft in the nearby ledge, which obscured most of the mountains. He could see the peak of a single giant. It was set in a background of bright blue sky. The peak itself was capped with white that seemed almost pale blue, growing darker into a purplish hue as the mountain grew thicker and more massive toward the base.

He turned and did not look back again.

*　　　　*　　　　*

Von Berkow was moving quickly, surely. It no longer mattered that the French guide was dead. When there are fresh footprints in the snow to follow, one does not need a guide. The edges of the footprints were straight and crisp.

They came to the ford. The captain plunged across without hesitation. The other two men stopped and considered the stream.

"What are you waiting for?" von Berkow asked, his voice harsh and angry.

"I want to make sure I don't fall in the water," the soldier said.

"You saw me cross. I didn't fall in."

"Maybe you were lucky."

"It is very shallow."

The lieutenant crossed, carefully, taking his time, placing each foot down slowly, making sure he was on solid footing before putting his weight on the foot. The soldier followed, tentative and fearful. Captain von Berkow paced up and down the bank, cursing under his breath, fuming at the delay. "Hurry up, you idiot!" he shouted at the soldier when he was halfway across. His shout almost caused the man to fall in the water.

The soldier took the last step out of the stream and immediately sat down on the bank. "I'm sorry, but I've always been afraid of drowning. I can't swim," he said.

The captain kicked him in the ribs.

"Get up, you lazy swine! What do you think this is, a rest camp?" He started down the path, again following the clear footprints, half walking, half running.

"Come on! Come on!" he shouted to the soldier, who was holding his side, and the lieutenant, who was regarding the captain with amazement and disgust.

The Basque led the Bergmans through a changing land. The sheer cliffs were being replaced by gentler, more rolling countryside. The snow was no longer a white blanket, now sporadic patches dotting the earth. The trees were more numerous.

They approached a grove of beech trees. As they passed around the grove, they came upon a herd of the wild, shaggy ponies found in the Pyrenees, the *pottokak*, whom the legends say are a species of prehistoric horse.

"Too bad we can't ride them," the girl said.

"They are too tiny," the boy said.

"And too wild," the Basque added. He pointed ahead, indicating an area near the base of a small hill. "My cabin is there. Less than a mile."

"Let's go," the boy said. His face had a bluish tint, and his teeth were chattering. "I'm freezing, and the water is starting to become ice."

The Basque threw his arm about the boy's shoulder. "Only another mile. We will build a fire and thaw you out."

"Me, too," the girl said.

"We could all use a fire," Bergman agreed.

There was something new among them. They had made it all the way through the mountains. To the Basque the cabin represented the final proof they had made it. Once inside the cabin, they would be secure. They would have conquered the mountains.

They moved forward, and it was easier now because it was simply a matter of going a mile. A purely physical task.

There was a lightness in their steps. It was almost as if they were starting a journey instead of coming to the end of one. Bergman and the girl smiled as they moved along, half trotting to keep up with the Basque. The boy tried to smile, but his teeth kept chattering, and he couldn't make his mouth obey.

They smile, the Basque thought, and that is unusual after such a journey. What is more unusual is that I feel like smiling myself. And for what reason? Because I have come back alive to the place I should never have left in the first place? Because now that Renoudot and Perea are both dead, I will not get the four thousand pesetas I was promised? Because God knows what has happened to my sheep while I have been away?

I have done what I have done, and it would be foolish to repent any of it because no matter what I think, I cannot change it or erase it or do it any other way than the way it has been done. We are trapped into being what we are by the deeds we have done.

They froze in their tracks when they heard the sound of rifle fire.

It was not over.

Lieutenant Reincke's heart pounded, and his face was red as he trotted behind the SS captain. The young soldier followed close behind his heels, panting and wheezing. They had been running ever since they had crossed the ford.

The man is insane, the lieutenant thought. From the beginning he had known the captain was a fanatic, a dedicated lunatic when it came to duty. But it was more than that. Von Berkow's desire to capture the Jew was unnatural, an obsession that rendered everything else meaningless. He reminds me of a child, the lieutenant thought, a spoiled child who has his mind set on a particular sweet, and if he is told he cannot have it, he will throw himself on the ground and cry and scream and turn red as a beet and threaten to hold his breath until he bursts. A spoiled child, yes, but far more serious. There was a madness in the man's eyes, a craziness that flashed on and off in a split second.

Why the hell am I running along behind this man, panting like a dog, chasing a single Jew? I am an army officer. I have been trained to command troops, to lead them into battle, to outwit the enemy with superior military tactics. That is what I have been trained to do, and here I am, following a *policeman* as if I were nothing more than one of his Alsatians. I might as well be wearing a collar and chain.

The captain stopped abruptly. He pointed toward a grove of trees. "Look," he whispered. "There on the other side of the trees."

The lieutenant peered through the trees and saw movement. The object moved again. He smiled and turned toward the captain. The captain's rifle was on his shoulder, and he was squeezing the trigger.

The lieutenant was about to say "stop." He was too late. The captain squeezed the trigger, and the rifle fired.

CRAAAAACK!!

The captain shouted in triumph and leapt forward. He stopped when he came around the trees and saw what it was he had shot.

"I tried to tell you," the lieutenant said.

The captain looked at him with murderous eyes and then back at the ground where the dead pony was still quivering. His victim. A pony. One of the shaggy *pottokak.*

"It doesn't matter," the captain said.

The lieutenant was angry, and his words hissed out between clenched teeth. "But it does matter."

"What do you mean?"

"You see something move, and you shoot it. A pony, a harmless pony. You will kill anything, and it doesn't matter. It doesn't make any difference to you what you kill."

"Shut up!"

"No. I will not shut up. The chase is over, do you understand? Finished, done. Stoecker and I are going back."

The captain's voice was low but filled with anger and rage. "I am in charge here, and I am ordering you to obey my orders."

The lieutenant shook his head. "No," he said.

The low voice went to a shrill shout. "You don't understand! I am in charge here! I give the orders!"

"It is you who do not understand," the lieutenant said, all his anger for this man pouring out. "Do you know where we are? In Spain, Captain, Spain. Do you know we are not supposed to be here? We are here illegally. What do you think will happen in Berlin if the Spanish government protests that German soldiers cross their border and chase people through their countryside? Aren't you aware that Spain has an agreement with Berlin? We must get out of here."

"I am not leaving without Bergman."

"Then get him by yourself. I am going back." He turned and started walking back in the direction they had come from. "Stoecker," he said to the soldier, "the chase is over. Come with me."

The soldier began to obey and froze at the sound of the rifle.

CRAAAAACK!!!!

The force of the bullet in his spine knocked the lieutenant forward, and he fell facedown into a patch of snow. The captain walked up to him and turned his body over with the end of his boot.

He was alive, barely, and the light of life was fading quickly in his eyes.

Captain von Berkow smiled.

"By now you should know enough to obey orders, Lieutenant," he said pleasantly. "Good hunting in Valhalla."

The terrified soldier stood with his mouth open. The captain looked at him. "Follow me," he said.

The soldier fell in behind the captain without a word. He glanced back at the lieutenant several times, but the pace set by the captain was very fast, and he almost stumbled. He forgot about looking back and moved after the captain.

Lieutenant Helmut Reincke felt the life draining from his body. The bullet must have hit my spine, he thought in a very objective way, hit or grazed my spine because it has paralyzed me. I am grateful it did not hit my brain because it would have deprived me of these last thoughts.

Now what shall I think about with my last thoughts? Something from my childhood? Something from my university days? Happy thoughts about my friends and the songs we sang and the beer we drank and the girls we knew?

Or shall I think about my family? My mother and father and the old grandmother with the wart on the side of her nose, the wonderful old lady who always smelled the same as a fresh-baked cake, shall I think about her?

Or Hilde, beautiful Hilde? The girl I probably would have made my wife, shall I think about her?

When you only have a few moments left on earth, it becomes important to think about the right things.

To die with a smile on your face.

To have peace of mind while the body fades away.

Valhalla, the captain had said. Was there a Valhalla? Where German warriors went when their mortal days were done? Was it a place for all German warriors, or only the heroes?

Maybe I should be thinking about Valhalla, thinking about the future instead of the past.

And while he was deciding what to spend his last moments thinking about, he died.

22

They stood looking back in the direction of the rifle fire. They were in Spain, and it was supposed to be over.

But it was not.

Isaac Bergman's face twitched. He looked at the Basque and then at each of his children. "Enough," he said angrily. "They want me, not you. I am going back. They can have me."

"No!" Leah said.

"We will get away," Samuel said. "Please don't go back."

The shepherd stared at Bergman for a few moments. Finally he said, "Go in that direction. Stay off the snow and leave no tracks. Near the bottom of the path you will come to a grave. Wait there for me."

"And you?"

The Basque smiled grimly. There was determination on his face. "I am going to put an end to this."

Bergman stepped forward. He spoke lamely, weakly. "You do not have to do this. I am the one they want."

"And I am the one who says they will not get you," the Basque said.

Leah stepped forward and impulsively reached out and took the Basque's hand. Their eyes met. They did not speak. The Basque withdrew his hand gently. He turned without a word and walked swiftly out beyond the cover of the trees. His feet made clear tracks in the fresh snow. He disappeared over the knoll, and the others turned and went down the mountain toward the grave, carefully stepping in the snowless patches beneath the trees. In moments they vanished from view.

Gunther von Berkow left the dying lieutenant in a pool of his own blood. He would have shot him again, given him the coup de grace, except it occurred to him it might benefit the lieutenant to have a few minutes for reflection before he died. He would make a better corpse if he knew *why* he had died.

He trotted forth for several hundred meters, and suddenly the tracks of his quarry were clear and unmistakable. He did not notice there was only one set of tracks. He began to trot faster, the soldier following, panting, his breath coming in gasps. Private Erich Stoecker tried his best to match the pace set by the captain. He trotted doggedly, his mouth open, his tongue darting in and out. His rifle began to feel as if it weighed a hundred pounds.

He was dazed by what was happening. He was a simple man, a soldier trained to obey orders. A simple man who had become a soldier to escape the grimness of existence with a poverty-stricken family. He found army life tolerable if not always luxurious, orderly if not sensible. But the killing of the lieutenant had dazed him. It had happened so suddenly. Where was the order in that? A German officer shooting another German officer in the back! Impossible!

The captain was getting farther ahead with every step. My God, Private Stoecker thought, I must keep up with him, or he will kill me, too!

The Basque was traveling rapidly. He had moved back toward the mountains, making no attempt to cover his tracks. He stopped once and listened. When he heard the sounds of pursuit, he resumed his rapid pace.

He came around a large outcropping of boulders and stopped when he saw the face of the glacier.

It was a small glacier. The pile of ice and new snow gave off a bright glare. Bits of crushed rock and stone dotted the face of the ice wall.

The glacier comprised one side of a narrow V-shaped ravine. It was wider at the front and narrowed down to nothing at the far end. The Basque ran rapidly down the ravine until he came to the end, which was a jumble of rock, snow, ice, and crushed trees. It was an old glacier, and he knew it well.

When he reached the end of the ravine, he turned and looked back, shielding his eyes from the glare of the sun on the ice. He began to climb the wall of rock opposite the ice face. In a few minutes he had reached the top, and looking across, his practiced eye quickly noticed the piles of new snow on top of the older ice.

He unslung his rifle and checked the breech. He pulled back the bolt and dropped a cartridge into the open mechanism. He pushed the bolt forward, and the bullet disappeared into the firing chamber.

He stood in the open, looking back down the ravine.

Captain von Berkow and the soldier rounded the pile of boulders. The soldier stumbled, and the captain shouted at him to get up. The two men continued down the ravine. They did not look up and see the Basque standing in the open at the top of the ravine. The captain was too intent following the footprints, and the soldier was exhausted.

When the Germans had come two-thirds of the way down the ravine, the Basque raised his rifle to his shoulder and aimed across at the face of the icewall. He pulled the trigger, and the gun fired, sending the bullet crashing into the other side.

A crack appeared where the bullet hit. The reverberations of the explosion rocked and slammed back and forth across the walls of the ravine. A chunk of ice broke loose from the top and plunged downward, taking the loose snow that had been on top of it.

Von Berkow looked up and saw the Basque. He whipped his rifle to his shoulder and pulled the trigger.

The bullet hit the Basque in the fleshy part of his shoulder. The impact caused him to grunt, and he stepped back a pace.

The reverberations caused by the second bullet seemed to multiply the rumblings until they merged into a dull roar.

The soldier, Stoecker, looked up in fear and screamed as he saw the wall of ice cracking along its length. One chunk tumbled down, and then another and another until a huge slab seemed to slowly ease itself away from the wall and plunge down toward the two men at the bottom. Von Berkow leaped forward, but he was too late, and a pile of loose snow from the top fell on him and buried him.

The anguished scream of the soldier was silenced as several tons of ice and stone bits crashed down on top of him.

Great slabs of ice and snow continued to plummet down for a few moments, and then they ceased. There was a silence punctuated only by the shifting wisps of white powder that filled the air.

The Basque looked down into the open ravine that had become a grave. There was no expression on his face. He touched the place where the bullet had hit, and his fingers came away smeared with blood.

He turned and walked along the ridge of the ravine back toward the Bergman family.

23

Isaac Bergman sat on the ground near the grave. His children sat a little distance away. All were lost in their thoughts.

Bergman was thinking about his children. Was the nightmare over? Or was it only beginning? What would happen to him? What would happen to the children?

No matter what else happened, they must have a chance to live in a world free of these Nazi murderers. They must have a chance to live in a world where a man is judged by what he does, not by what religion he inherited from his ancestors. A child is born, and he is given a place in life by his mother and father. He is given a color and a God to worship. He is given a name. He is given his language and his prejudices. Half the things he will ever be in life are given to him by the accident of birth.

And all children are blameless because not one of them asked to be born into this world. Not one of them *requested* to be a German or a Jew or a Catholic or an Englishman. They were born, and they were given no say in these matters. Nothing a man did in life was as important as being born because without this there could be nothing more.

The event that is the most important in our lives is also the event over which we have absolutely no control.

What chance do we have, he thought; no wonder we become pessimists, eternal pessimists.

But I refuse to *remain* a pessimist. I could have been dead, but I am not, and this experience will not be wasted, he promised himself. If I live, I will be Lazarus risen from the dead. Every day that I live I will consider a bonus from the hand of God. And I will not squander a week of this time, a day or a minute.

The fight against the Nazi madness is only beginning. It is still a whisper in a darkened night, a flame that burns so low it almost cannot be seen. But the flame lives, and it burns, and it will grow and build until it is no longer a tiny flame but a proper fire and then a roaring blaze and finally a flaming holocaust that consumes everything in its path, and it will burn the house of the Nazis to the ground and burn their flesh and pulverize their bones and etherize their black souls. "As you have done, so it will be done to you," said Hillel. And so it would be.

He would make arrangements to go to Portugal as soon as possible. From Portugal it would be possible to make his escape to England or America or Canada. He had many friends in the universities of these countries, and he would call upon them to help him in his crusade against the Nazis.

It had become his cause, his only cause and his only

ambition. His other ambitions were gone, as dead as the wife who lay frozen on the side of a mountain.

His daughter Leah sat a few feet away. She was confused. The death of her mother had been a great blow, but it was difficult for her to keep thinking of her mother. Instead, she thought of the shepherd. He was not the sort of man she had been used to meeting, yet she felt strangely drawn to him. She tried to dismiss the feeling as one of gratitude, only she knew that wasn't true.

She heard a noise nearby and looked up.

"I am here."

Leah smiled with relief when she saw the shepherd. She stood up and went toward him. "Oh," she said with a gasp, "you're hurt."

"It is nothing."

Bergman and his son both rose. A smile of happiness spread over the boy's face.

"The Germans?" Bergman asked.

"Dead," the Basque said. He stopped and looked at the grave.

Bergman came up beside him. He looked at the grave and then at the Basque. "Your wife?" he asked.

Erno Urquijo nodded.

He was looking at the mound of earth, but his eyes did not see it. A vision of a young girl was before him. The face of the young girl he had taken to the cemetery on the day of their wedding, an old Basque tradition, to remind themselves they would one day lie side by side in the earth for all eternity.

I came close to lying in the earth, he thought, but not by your side. I have also come to a new wisdom.

I have been with this family. I have seen a woman love

her family so much she was able to give her life that they might be spared. I have seen a man understand that this sacrifice must not be wasted, and he left her unburied on the mountain to become a meal for wolves and vultures in the spring thaw.

A boy with a crippled leg and a desperate need to survive has made me feel ashamed.

A girl with the courage of a man and a will that bows to nothing has made me proud of another human being.

My eyes are opening from deep sleep.

I am not dead and can no longer act as a dead man, no longer live in the past, no longer be a spectator whose life is a passing dream.

I am flesh and blood, and I must be with flesh and blood. I must hear the conversations of men and the laughter of women. I must listen to the hopes and dreams of people who have not given up because they know they are alive. There are problems with living, there are pains, but that is the way of life, to have problems and pains.

Only the dead are free from pain.

The vision faded.

He looked away from the mound of earth. "My cabin is this way," he said, starting down the hill.

After the Basque had left the ravine with the buried Germans, a mound of snow stirred. It moved again, and a hand came out from beneath the powdered death. Finally a clump of snow moved, and the face of Captain von Berkow emerged.

It was cut and bleeding. His cap was gone. With a great effort he struggled to bring his body out of the snow. He kicked one leg free and then brought out the other arm. It was still clutching the rifle.

He looked up at the last place he had seen the Basque. He stood up and moved toward the end of the ravine. He did not bother to look back at the grave of his companion.

24

The Basque led the others to his cabin. The roof was covered with a layer of snow. The gates to the pen were open as he had left them. The sheep were in the pen, some of them ambling through the narrow chute that was used when they were being milked. A deep, low growl menaced him as he approached the gate.

"Bai, bai," the Basque said, and the growling stopped. "Bai, bai."

The *Komondorok* came from the side of the pen. He patted each on the head. He looked at his house with its attached barn, the heavy beams smeared and protected with ox blood.

Everything was the way he had left it.

The dogs growled again. Bergman and his son and daughter were standing in the gateway.

"Quiet," the Basque said, and the dogs subsided. He

pointed to a place by the side of the gate, and the dogs went over and lay down. They never took their eyes off the strangers. A little sheep dog came racing out of the barn and hurled himself at the Basque. "Hey, hey," the man said with a smile as the little dog licked his face. The big dogs ignored the scene. One of them yawned.

"This is your home?" Leah asked.

"Yes."

She was surprised. "You said it was a cabin. This is so much nicer than I had imagined," she said, admiring the sturdy house. It was made of stone and strengthened with heavy beams. The tile roof was covered with white snow, which matched the whitewashed walls of the house.

"It is very handsome," Bergman said.

"Are these your sheep?" Samuel asked.

"All of them."

"You are a fortunate man to live in such a peaceful place," Isaac Bergman said. "I have never lived like this. I often wondered what it would be like to live in a world of such peace."

"It is not an easy life," Erno said.

"But there is not great competition or strife," Bergman said. "You work at your own pace and set your own goals. Most of us are not that fortunate."

The Basque agreed. He had begun to understand more about this man in the past few days. He was wise, and despite his seeming helplessness the man understood many things about the world.

"Can we have a fire, please," Samuel begged.

The Basque nodded and turned toward the house.

CRAAAAACK!!!!

They froze. They looked in the direction of the gate, and their blood ran cold. A German, dressed in white, was coming toward them, a rifle in his hands.

The Basque's rifle was strapped to his back. If he tried to take it off, the German could easily shoot him. He stood motionless.

The German paused ten feet outside the gate, his rifle pointed toward them. The Basque looked at the man and saw it was the SS captain who had inspected the Gypsy caravan at St. Limoux. Except now the man had an ugly gash on his forehead, and the blood was clotting. His lip was torn, and he trembled from the adrenaline coursing through his veins. The German looked ready to explode, his eyes bright, fierce. And then the man did a strange thing.

He smiled.

The Basque was thinking it might be better to at least try to get the rifle off his back. If he died, he would have at least died trying instead of standing like a helpless tool.

And then he saw something in the corner of his eye that changed his mind.

He did not need the rifle.

"Bergman?" Captain von Berkow asked.

"I am Bergman."

Von Berkow smiled. "I almost didn't recognize you. The last time I saw you, I believe you were a Gypsy."

Bergman said nothing.

Von Berkow regarded the others. "Ahhh, the pretty Gypsy girl. Your father seems to have made a remarkable recovery," he said sarcastically.

His eyes stopped on the Basque. "And you, I have bad news for you. It's about your brother."

The Basque said nothing.

"You do remember your brother, don't you? The fat one? Well, he had the bad fortune to die. The cause was a half-dozen bullets through the heart."

The ones in the yard said nothing.

"No one has anything to say, is that it?" the captain said, the words coming between deep, heavy breaths.

"Who is to be the first to die?" he asked, keeping his eye on the Basque. He had noticed the rifle strapped to the man's back.

"You are going to kill us?" Bergman asked.

"Not you. The others."

"Take me. I will go with you and cause no trouble. But let the others live. I beg you."

Von Berkow sneered. "Just like a Jew to beg. Don't waste your time. Now let's stop this nonsense. Who is to be the first to die?"

"At least let the children live," the Basque said.

Von Berkow studied the man. "What do you care about these Jews? If they didn't need you to help them, they would spit in your ugly face and laugh at you."

"Perhaps. I ask for their lives in any case."

The smile on Von Berkow's face faded. "You are in no position to ask for anything."

The Basque looked at him very deliberately. He shouted one word. Very clearly. "Wolf."

There was movement on von Berkow's left. He turned, but he did not turn quickly enough. He tried to bring his rifle up, but a large white blur slammed into him, and he felt a powerful set of jaws grab his arm. The teeth crunched through flesh and bone, and he screamed and tried to pull away.

Another white blur struck him high on the chest with great force. He was slammed back on the ground, and the rifle fell to the side. The jaws holding his arm relaxed, and he pulled his arm free. He screamed again as the jaws struck lower and bit into the fleshy thigh, piercing through the clothing and the skin and stabbing deeply enough to crunch bone.

It was a dog! What kind of dog? He had never seen a dog like this. No, not a dog, there were two of them!

The dogs were growling fiercely. He began to beat his fists on the head of the one that had his thigh. The other dog lunged at his head, and von Berkow managed to duck. It was not enough to prevent the dripping jaws from raking the side of his cheek, leaving red lines that immediately filled with blood and began running down his face. The teeth of the dog caught his ear as they passed and tore most of it off.

The dog fell past him with a whine of rage and frustration, pausing slightly to shake his head and spit out the bloody pieces of flesh that had been the man's ear.

Von Berkow flailed at the dog. As he did, the other dog, the one who held the thigh in his jaws, released his hold and lunged forward, crunching his jaws down on the man's groin. The huge teeth slashed through the heavy clothing and closed with tremendous power on the man's testicles. The man screamed, and the dog began throwing his head from side to side, tearing the manhood from von Berkow's body.

The captain's scream was the scream of a lost soul entering through the gates of hell. With a lunge born of a last gasp of demoniac strength, he tried to raise himself up. He placed his arms behind him and then realized his mistake. The other dog, the other white blur, had come around in front of him, and the jaws with the awesome teeth were at his face.

While the one dog was tearing his guts apart, the jaws of the other one went about the man's throat and ripped it out. The jaws flashed a second time and began shaking what was left of the throat. Blood splattered over the snow. Slivers of bone and globs of membrane stained the white earth. The fierce growls mingled with the man's death shrieks.

The sounds of death echoed through the hills.

The dogs stopped.

The Bergman family was stunned. The dogs had killed with a ferocity they had never seen.

"What a way to die," Samuel said in awe.

Bergman put his arm about his son. "Perhaps we should go into the cabin."

Leah stood in silence next to the Basque.

"It is over," Erno said.

He filled his lungs with the sharp mountain air.

A jagged flash of lightning cut the sky in two, and a sonorous clap of thunder rolled over the hills and valleys and caused the earth to tremble.

The world waited in the grayness.

The first flakes fell from the darkening sky.

It was to be a big storm, and a long one.

Winter was upon the earth.

The Basque turned and walked toward his cabin with Leah.

The day was done.

EPILOGUE

In September 1943, the Germans captured a Spanish Basque in the foothills of the French Pyrenees. They suspected him of being one of the men who smuggled refugees across the mountains. They held him for questioning. He was incarcerated in the back room of a bakery, awaiting the arrival of the Gestapo interrogator.

Before the Gestapo man arrived, the bakery was blown up by the French Underground and the Spanish Basque disappeared. The local authorities, to cover up their blunder, claimed the Spanish Basque had been killed in the blast.

The Gestapo investigators, after carefully examining the wreckage in the bakery and finding no trace of the Basque, knew the report was false. They allowed the record to stand, however, not wishing to cause trouble for other Germans.

The report was forwarded to Paris and then to Berlin with the information that the Spanish Basque, suspected of smuggling refugees, was dead.

They never did learn what became of him.

ABOUT THE AUTHOR

Bruce Nicolaysen spent 15 years as a copywriter and advertising executive before becoming a full-time writer. He has also written the screenplay for PERILOUS PASSAGE, his first novel, as well as several other films. Since 1961, he has lived on the West Coast, currently in Los Angeles.

EBANO

Alberto Vazquez-Figueroa

Now filmed as **ASHANTI**

Nadia was beautiful. Sophisticated. And black.
Which was why she became a kidnap-target for
the slave-traders who even today still ply their
brutal profession between the horn of Africa
and oil-rich Arabia. Nadia was a fabulous black
jewel, fit decoration for the closely-guarded
harem of a millionaire sheik. So they took her.

But Nadia was not destined to disappear
without search or trace. For she was married to
a European, British photographer David
Alexander. He was to travel the slave-routes,
gathering around him others who had blood
debts to settle with the merchants of bondage –
in a grim, relentless quest to find the wife he
loved . . .

EBANO is the enthralling, shocking and
savagely authentic novel that reveals the
unbelievable truth:
SLAVERY – OF THE CRUELLEST KIND –
FLOURISHES TODAY!

GENERAL FICTION/FILM TIE IN   95p

0 7221 3496 7

MIDNIGHT EXPRESS

Billy Hayes and William Hoffer

Now a major film from Columbia Pictures

What's a nice guy like you doing in a place like this?

For Billy Hayes, 1970 was a horrifying year. It was the year when he tried to smuggle 4lbs of hashish from Istanbul back to his home in America. It was the year when he was arrested at Istanbul airport, tried, and sentenced to thirty years in a Turkish jail.

For five years he suffered the filth, brutality and degradation of imprisonment in an environment of hellish squalor, while his family fought in vain to secure his release. Finally, in desperation, he made a daring escape-bid and incredibly, the bid succeeded!

This is the astounding true story, told in Billy Hayes's own words, of those five years of living hell and of the harrowing ordeal of his time on the run. Vivid, realistic without being morbid, it is a classic story of survival and human endurance, told with humour, intelligence and total honesty.

AUTOBIOGRAPHY/FILM TIE-IN   95p

0 7221 0471 5

A MAN CALLED INTREPID:
The Secret War 1939-1945

The International bestseller by William Stevenson

A Man Called Intrepid tells for the first time the full story of British Security Co-Ordination, the International Allied intelligence agency of World War Two whose work has been a closely guarded secret for the past thirty years. Here are top-level inside accounts of crucial wartime undercover operations including:

- [ ] The breaking of the German *Enigma* code
- [ ] The assassination of Heydrich
- [ ] The race for the atomic bomb
- [ ] Surveillance and sabotage of Nazi V1 and V2 rocket sites
- [ ] The raids on the French coast that made the Normandy landings possible
- [ ] Anglo-American co-operation in the sinking of the *Bismarck*
- [ ] The organization of resistance movements throughout Europe
- [ ] The intelligence stratagems that delayed the Nazi invasion of Russia

Writen with full access to all the British Security Co-Ordination papers and with the full co-operation of BSC's director, the man code-named INTREPID, William Stevenson's internationally bestselling book is a uniquely important piece of modern secret history. It is also tremendously exciting to read.

"A work of profound historical importance . . . a great adventure story, wherein fact is more sensational than fiction . . . more stimulating than any record I have seen about the infinite complexity of modern warfare" DAVID BRUCE (*FORMER OSS CHIEF AND LATER US AMBASSADOR TO BRITAIN*)

BIOGRAPHY/WAR   £1.75

0 7221 8158 2